Trapped

Trapped

Gren Gaskell

Trapped
Gren Gaskell

Published by Aspect Design 2017
Malvern, Worcestershire, United Kingdom.

Designed, printed and bound by Aspect Design
89 Newtown Road, Malvern, Worcs. WR14 1PD
United Kingdom
Tel: 01684 561567
E-mail: allan@aspect-design.net
Website: www.aspect-design.net

All Rights Reserved.

Copyright © 2017 Gren Gaskell

Gren Gaskell has asserted his moral right
to be identified as the author of this work.

The right of Gren Gaskell to be identified as the author
of this work has been asserted in accordance with
Section 77 of the Copyright, Designs and Patents Act 1988.

This book is sold subject to the condition that it shall not, by way of trade or otherwise, be lent, resold, hired out or otherwise circulated without the publisher's prior consent in any form of binding or cover other than that in which it is published and without a similar condition including this condition being imposed on the subsequent purchaser.

A copy of this book has been deposited with the British Library Board

ISBN 978-1-912078-66-0

*To my wife who has made me as I am,
the luckiest, the happiest of men.*

With grateful thanks to Jeanne for her patience

HIDING

It's cold in here but it's better than being out there. I hide here sometimes when they get on to me. I know they'll find me, but there's not many places to hide in school. Hiding places, you know, really good, secret places, are hard to find, that's why they're good, isn't it? There's one across the other side of the old corporation tip and I've used that many times. Only one other person knows it's there and she won't tell anybody. Jane can keep a secret as good as I can.

I suppose I've always been a hider. When I was little, I mean a very little kid, I thought I could hide by closing my eyes. If I couldn't see them I thought they couldn't see me. I must have been very stupid. A lot of people here think I'm very stupid now. They expect little kids to hide, but not a lad of fifteen years old.

I thought I could hear somebody then, but it was the water system making a noise. I'm safe for a bit longer.

They sent me to see a man who was an expert in this, kids who need to hide. He tried to suggest that I was hiding from my brothers and sisters. I think that was a blind. He really wanted to know how I felt about my mam and dad. He asked a load of questions, but I never told him the truth. Although I do hate him, my dad, I didn't say about why I do it. Perhaps that's why it didn't do any good. Perhaps if I had told the man he might have been able to help.

I could have said about my dad knocking us about and the cruel games he played with animals and how I hated him, whether he was drunk or sober.

The expert might have cured me if I'd have said something. I know for some people it must be a kind of illness—that's obvious even to me who does it—but I couldn't confide in him.

I've never talked to anybody about it. I don't expect I ever shall.

Does everybody have secrets? I bet they do. It's just that some things are more secret than others.

I have got some ordinary secrets, you know, like we've all got, but what makes me different is the big ones. My big secrets that nobody else knows about. The noises at night at home, and what I saw with my own eyes at the hut, and what has been happening to me since.

Most kids think that hiding the fact that they smoke is a big secret. Pooh, that's nothing. Or what they've done with a girl, or a boy for that matter. These things are all secrets that we can boast about. I couldn't brag about what had happened to me, not even to my own brothers.

Don and Dick had given up on me early on, and my sisters were too secretive themselves to be of any help. None of them hardly ever speak to me.

I was always different though, as long as I can remember I didn't fit in. Was that why all these things happened to me?

Every single thing is as clear as if it was yesterday, and I go over it all the time. I've even made a few notes so that I will never forget the details, but if anybody ever reads what I've written they wouldn't understand what the writing is about. I made very sure of that.

I don't suppose I'll ever be able to tell anybody, except perhaps when I'm older and meet somebody who will marry me. Then I'll probably tell that one person, but only on the promise, the sacred vow, that they will never, ever share the secret. If I don't meet that person, that one person, then I shall definitely take these secrets to the grave and no one will ever know what I've seen.

I've spent a lot of my life hiding. Mam thought, when I was little, it was a game that I would grow out of and I expect that's what would have happened if it weren't for different things. Then she got really angry when I kept on with it, and because I wouldn't talk to her about what I was doing. I got a lot of beltings then. She thought she could knock it out of me and had a good try to do that. I suppose she was hitting me for my own good, but it didn't work. How could it?

Dad belts me for no reason other than the fact that he don't like me.

Footsteps. I'm holding my breath. They've gone to the urinal so, whoever it is, they aren't looking for me.

The teacher said last week that if I kept on doing this they would leave me to stay a whole day. She meant they wouldn't try to find me. I didn't answer. As far as I'm concerned that would be great.

He's gone now, that person who came in. I could tell it was a man, not one of the boys.

It's always Miss Barton who comes to find me now; they never send a man teacher.

The longest I have ever hidden was the whole of one afternoon and evening, from about one o'clock till gone eight that night. Mam said she was about to send for the police, but she wouldn't have. I know that's the last thing she would do and she knows I know it. That is a kind of unspoken pact between us. No outsiders. Not the police, neighbours, not anybody ever again.

The school got her to agree to the psychology man seeing me, but she could tell I hadn't said anything to him as soon as I came out of his office and she was pretending to be angry with me in front of him.

'Why didn't you open up to the man?' she asked, before he'd even left the room, sounding just as if she really did want me to say things. I looked at the man's face and he was looking very troubled about it all. I got the feeling he had guessed was what was happening at home. He was hoping I would tell him things about Mam and Dad, but I kept the promise I had made to myself and I said nothing.

I felt sorry for the specialist in a way. It's his job to help people and not everybody wants that kind of help. I just couldn't see how he would be able to help me.

Miss Barton used to say I was my own worst enemy. Perhaps she was right then, I did seem to cause of lot of trouble for myself. But that was because they didn't understand what had happened. She doesn't say it now though.

If I was to speak to anyone about my secret before I get to be proper grown up it would have to be Miss Barton. She has been very kind to me since I came to this school. It's as if she has guessed my secrets—but she can't possibly know. She doesn't question me, but she has made it very clear that, when I'm ready to talk, I can always talk to her. I think it might be a kind of a trap, to lure me into a sense of security and then get me to talk. Well, I would talk to her if I was going to talk to somebody, but I won't.

It is cold in here but early on I learned to take precautions. I always wear my thickest jumper to come to school, so I'm ready. That's one of the things that got the bullying going. Kids pick on kids who are nesh, and wearing thick clothes in all weathers does make me stand out a bit. We all wear second-hand clothes at our house, it's something we have to do. Some places I hide in are colder than this and these lavs are quite cold. I once hid in the back of a lorry. It had been carrying animals of some sort and I got covered in poo. I didn't half stink and the man who discovered me there thought I'd been forced to lie in the mess by a bully. I didn't say anything. That was early on and I was learning not to draw too much attention to myself when I got caught. 'Come out, we know you're there.' I always hated to hear them shout that.

'Let them think what they want to think,' my mam said, and I'm sure that is the best thing.

I wonder if this is the time when I could try to reach up to the trapdoor in the lavatory ceiling. I am growing quite fast now and I'm certainly taller than the last time I tried it. I'm over five-foot-six now and what's happening to me proves that I look a lot older than my age.

If I could climb into there nobody would find me, ever; I'll give it a go. Onto the seat and, yes, wahay, I can reach the trapdoor. Gently, push it up, gently. I've learned to do things quietly. It's loose and I can move it to one side. There. Now find somewhere for my hands to hold on to and I can pull myself up. This is what I practise on the bars for, lifting my weight by pulling on my arms and it's given me a decent shaped body, a thirty-inch waist and almost a thirty-eight-inch chest.

That's it, I'm up.

It's lovely and dark now the trapdoor is back in place. There is a small light though, it's coming in through a tile that's slipped, but it's not much. Funny really, when I was little, I was terrified of the dark and I would lie awake for hours listening to the house creaking and the other noises; it was the other noises that frightened me most. Don made me promise not to tell anybody what we could hear. Dad went mad and gave Don a really savage belting when he did mention the noises coming from the girls' room.

When I took to hiding proper I realised what a friend the dark was.

They haven't lagged this space. That causes problems, that fibre glass stuff. I had to have ointment for my skin from the doctor once after lying on insulation. Mam made up a story for him because he said he'd never seen such a mess on a body. I bet he had though, being a doctor. I wonder why anybody would want to be a doctor. I never wanted to do anything or be anything really.

Mam used to say, 'Give him time, he's a slow learner, that's all.'

She's got no idea what I have learnt.

When I was little I used to try to talk to her. I would say, 'Listen to this Mam,' and read a bit from a book that I was so excited about and she would say, 'That's nice, dear,' even when what I read was horrible and frightening, and wasn't nice at all. 'That's nice, dear,' I can hear her saying it now in this little space, in the dark.

So I stopped telling her things and she doesn't really know why I hide and she never will, not properly. I sometimes think she is guessing.

That doesn't stop her pretending to people that she does know, to the doctor and such. She puts on this air of understanding that lasts until they've gone.

She is definitely the last person I would ever tell.

Dad couldn't care less about my hiding and I'm not sure Mam tells him much about anything.

I wonder if Miss Barton would understand. Would she believe I was telling the truth? Because of what's happened between us, I am tempted to really open up to her.

Mam asked me the other day if I was aware of the effect my behaviour had on other people. *My behaviour*, that's what she called it. Like starting to wet the bed again.

Some time ago, when I was not so rational, and before my lucky break, I used to plan how I could die. Once, when I was very angry, I planned a way to go and take them with me. Mam and Dad I mean. It was in a space like this where I could have some poison, take some, then fall into a tank that supplied the water to our house and that would poison them two as well. Then I thought about Don and the rest of the family, so I decided not to do it. Now I just accept the fact that things are as they are, so these are my secrets and mine alone.

When the picture of the man was in the paper, and I know it was definitely him, I felt sorry for the woman and I still don't think any of it can have been her fault.

That time when they came to the hut I know that neither the men nor the woman saw me. They don't know that anybody saw what they did. They can't possibly suspect that there was anybody watching. Not there.

It was one of my very best hideouts and only me knew about it. In the roof-space there was just room for me. I don't think even I could scraum into that space now, I'd be too big. I could only get in then by lying on my belly but, when I did, I could see out of the side and down into the little room below through thin gaps in the planks. I could see if anybody was coming because there was only the one way through the thick brambles and I had a clear view to that side of the hut.

I've got no idea what it was built for. It was made of wood and was miles away from anywhere. Well, not miles, but a good half-hour walk if you walked fast. And I always walked fast and I even ran part of the way to get there because I didn't want to be followed. No one's ever followed me.

On that day, when the three of them turned up, I could hear them coming a long time before I saw them because of the noise. I'd seen Mam and Dad when they were drunk, so I knew straight away what condition these people were in. They laughed at the state of their clothes when they staggered into the clearing because they'd been torn on the brambles. The men were making a fuss about the woman's dress and pulling it about to show how much it had been ripped. One of the men had carried a blanket wrapped round his body. I thought it was to guard against the brambles. It wasn't. They looked surprised when they saw the hut, as if they didn't know it was there, but I knew this wasn't true about the woman. She already knew. I had found some fag ends when I had visited some days before and while they were there on that day she smoked the same sort. I know because I checked the make. She always stubbed the fags out when they were only half smoked and you could read part of the print.

Most lads would have been tempted to take some matches and smoke the dog ends, but not me. I have never been tempted to smoke. It's a very stupid thing to do and it doesn't make you look big, just stupid.

And lot of lads who found themselves up here now would want to crawl along to see if they could peep down into the girl's lav, but that's another difference. I don't hide to be sneaky and spy on folks. I just hide.

I wouldn't have spied on the folks who came to that hut, but the sounds they made were odd so I had a quick peep to check they weren't drowning in vomit, like I read in the paper about somebody who got drunk. Nobody was. They were making noises, but they were far from dead, so I lay and watched what they were doing and waited for them to go.

I knew it. Miss Barton has come in and she's calling my name. She only calls soft because she doesn't want the others to hear, but they know. My class can see I'm missing and they'll be having a laugh. It really doesn't bother me, honestly. I shall hide when I want to and whenever I get the chance.

I'm not sure what to do. If I give myself up while she's there she'll know that I can now climb up here because she's checked all the cubicles, so I think I'll wait till she's gone and get down and go home. Mam has given me my own key. She thought if she did that I wouldn't have to hide anywhere. She has no idea where I go now. My mother hasn't got a clue.

This is one good thing about living pretty close to school, it only took ten minutes to get home and I suppose I could ring the school now and say I was unwell. They can't fetch me back from home, I think that's against the law. Anyway, I can sit and read, that's what I like to do when I'm here alone; when the others are in, I go to the library and hide there in the books I read. They all think I'm weird, my brothers and sisters, but I'm not bothered now.

I seem to be the only one who does bother about the state of the house though. When I went with Jane to her house, and she invited me in, the difference was amazing. Her house was clean with nice, comfortable furniture. There were books, and little ornaments in a cabinet with a glass front. When I saw that I thought to myself, 'Well that wouldn't last long at our house when they started falling out with each other and throwing things.' There was carpet on the floor and everywhere was clean with no dust. You can write your name in the dust on the tops at our house, if you don't mind getting a beating that is and if you can find a top without something left on it. At Jane's house there was the same smell I know from the library. I learned after that it was furniture polish. We don't have that here at our house.

I have to be very careful when I bring my library books home; I usually hide them in case dad throws them on the fire. He threatened to do that when I asked him questions. He said I was getting too many daft ideas from all the reading.

When I was little I read all the Enid Blyton Famous Five books, now I read anything I can. I just like reading, especially stories. There's not much to laugh at in this house, but I have to laugh every time I read those by W. W. Jacobs. He wrote years and years ago and they are so easy to read. O Henry is brilliant too.

Here it is. I saved that page from the paper with the picture of the man to remember how he looks. I'm absolutely certain this is him. I got a good look at the three of them when they were standing looking at the hut and he was the one egging the woman on to be silly. She was making a fuss of the third man, teasing him, and this one in the picture was encouraging her to open the door. Through the gap in the boards, I could see the face of the second man when he looked round and he was just pretending to be surprised, I'm sure of that. I don't know if this man in the photo had been there before, but I'm pretty sure he hadn't. Then they started doing things. The three of them together. Things I had never read about or heard lads at school speak about. The three of them were doing things together.

This kitchen is the worst room in the house. Everything is sticky with dirt and nothing ever gets cleaned. It's a wonder we don't all get poisoned. That's better, I've washed a mug and made a drink of tea. We don't have coffee here. I did ask Mam if we could have some once and dad went spare.

'That's out of them bloody books,' he shouted at me. 'You get too many ideas you do, you little prat. And I can knock them out of you if you don't come down to earth.'

It might be a good idea if the house did get cleaned and we got some decent furniture, but none of us dare say so.

I know it seems strange, but I've never liked living here. It's as if I'm with the wrong family and perhaps that feeling is because of the books. When you read about families in books they aren't like mine at all.

Not that I feel despair or that sort of thing, more confused and surprised at what happens to me.

I just hide away from everything and everybody, that way I can't get into any trouble, not while I'm hiding. I know that sounds daft, but it's a fact. When I'm with people, no matter who they are, I end up in trouble. There is only one, just one, person who is the exception to this, but I'm certain that Jane's family don't like me to be too friendly with her and I can't blame them. Jane is lovely and clean, and she is always dressed nice.

But seeing what I saw when I was hiding at the hut would get me into very serious bother if anybody found out I was there. The police might even think I was part of it. My DNA must be all over that place and I know that's used a lot now to solve crimes.

It took over a year before it got into the news. I realise I should have done something about it, told somebody or something, but I wasn't really certain what had happened, and when it came out, I was too frightened.

On that day, three of them went in and only two came out. I waited and watched as the man and the woman edged away through the brambles. He had wrapped the blanket round the woman's body and was saying how pleased he was and how she had done good. When I climbed down into the tiny room, there he was, the same man who was in the photo months later.

He didn't look dead. In fact, I didn't think he was at first. I thought he was just asleep, so I began to creep past him to the door. He wasn't making a sound, not a sound, and I wasn't sure he was breathing. I felt safer then, so I looked closer at him, and I could see the rope round his neck and a piece of orange. Things from the game they had been playing. I couldn't make head nor tail of it, what had been happening, but whatever it was, it seemed to have gone wrong.

The man and woman who had left hadn't seemed upset though, and I couldn't make it out. I was even more confused than usual. I didn't know what to do. I did feel angry that somebody had found the hut, but very glad they hadn't discovered me in my hiding place in it. I did nothing. I just went home.

It was on the following Saturday that I went back. I was very careful. I crept up to the place on all fours and watched and listened for ages before deciding the coast was clear and crossed the grass to open the door. The man was gone.

Lying in the roof space that morning, I did wonder if it had been a dream. We all do that sometimes, think things are real when they aren't. But the fag ends had gone, all of them. That's when it was clear that somebody had been in and taken the man and cleaned up.

I didn't want to give up the hiding place. I thought that perhaps the man who had been left wasn't dead; he had just been drunk and breathing shallowly and he had gone home when he woke. Anyway, after that, I was always very careful when I did come back and crept about in case they were there. I didn't get careless, and a good job too.

One afternoon, ages later, when I had capped school, I went to the hut, and as I got close, I could hear a woman crying. It was her again. The same woman as before. I lay in the bracken a little way away from the hut watching her smoke and she kept looking at her watch and crying.

I think it was a little fly, there were a lot about where I was, that crept up my nose and made me sneeze.

She looked across to where I was hiding and said very calmly, 'Please, come out.' So I did. The look of relief on her face stopped me being frightened and she called me over to her. 'Come here and let me look at you, young man,' she said.

So I did. And that was how I got to know her. We sat on a tree trunk that lay on the edge of the clearing and she asked me lots of questions like when I had found the hut, and how, and what I was doing there.

I was ever so careful and said I'd never been before and was wandering through the wood when I smelled her smoke. She offered me a fag and then, when I said I didn't smoke, she said she wished she didn't either. I felt very sad for her because she was so unhappy, and I suppose that's why I held her hand. I just sat by her side and held her hand, and she squeezed mine as if she never wanted to let it go, and she asked me how old I was. When I said I was fifteen she was a bit puzzled and said I looked older than that. Then, when she said she wished I was, I didn't like to ask her why she had said it in case it wasn't for the reason I hoped, so I said I'd very soon be sixteen. We sat there for ages and I asked her if she was waiting for somebody. She shook her head and sniffled.

'I might come and live here,' she said after a while. I pointed out there was no electric or water or anything and she said, 'No, but there is a lot of something else, all this peace and quiet.'

And I didn't know what to say because I was feeling very . . . well, strange inside.

Perhaps she sensed how I was feeling because she let go of my hand, ran hers down my leg and said it was getting cooler and we should perhaps go inside the hut.

Then I did get nervous and wondered if she might murder me or something. But she didn't. Instead it was the most wonderful afternoon in all my life.

We were in the hut for two hours almost, and when we came out she said, 'A boy went into that hut, and a man came out,' and she laughed and told me I was her lovely young prince and we could meet here again if I wanted to.

When I said yes, I did, she said she could come back on the following Tuesday afternoon, but I was not to be too disappointed if she didn't turn up because sometimes she had to work. She explained that it was safest for us both if we didn't know where the other lived and I was glad she had said that. The thought of my Mam and Dad getting to know what had happened was very frightening, and the woman said it was her that was taking all the risk because of my age. I told her that I knew how to keep a secret and I would come back as often as I could and wait for her, and she said I was to be very careful and not tell a soul.

I realised that for something like this to happen to a schoolboy was so lucky that, even if I was the sort that blabbed, nobody would believe me. But I really did know how to keep a secret. If you tell just one person then you don't have a secret any more, and this, what had happened, was a big thing to keep secret. But I have.

When Tuesday came, and it took ages to come, it was raining, but I wasn't bothered. I should have been at school because the half term holiday had ended, but what boy would have gone to school on that day? I had never felt as excited as I had through that long week.

I could hardly sleep and I thought of nothing else. Just her and what had happened between us.

I went early on the Tuesday and, having spent all week thinking about it, decided not to use my hiding place in the hut's roof space. That place was my secret, and if she knew about it, she might put two and two together and figure out that I might have been there when the three of them came to the hut.

I was soaked when I found a spot to hide where I could see the little clearing in front of the hut, and by that time the rain was sailing down. I would have bet my life that there was no chance the woman would turn up. But she did.

I watched her push her way out of the wet bracken and walk toward the door of the hut. She was wearing a long waxed raincoat, and I heard her tap on the door while she said, 'It's me,' very quietly.

I waited a few seconds after she went in before coming out of my hiding place and as soon as she saw me she laughed. 'We'd better get you out of these wet clothes,' she said, and my heart was filling my chest so tight I could hardly breathe.

She said I should watch her undress. She said that because I made as if to look away when she started to take her clothes off. 'I want to see you watch,' she said. And she wasn't smiling. She looked very serious.

Here in the quiet I can relive that second time. Perhaps it was even better than the first because she seemed more certain about things. What to do and that. At one stage, for a few seconds, she seemed to go berserk; it was a bit frightening because she was making the strange noises I had heard her make when the three of them were together in that same place. But I was only a very tiny bit frightened because it was unbelievably exciting.

That second time she said she had to rush and we only stayed a bit less than an hour, but she said we could meet again on the Saturday.

As she was leaving she took a five-pound note from her purse and tucked it into the top of my trousers. 'Don't expect this every time, but I want you to have it today,' she said, and then pretended to let go of it and had a little fumble round the bottom of my belly.

Saturday meant I did not have to wait a week. It seemed like it though. It seemed a lot longer than a week, longer than a month, or a year. I could hardly sleep, and although I went to school, because my mam threatened to lock me in the house if I didn't, I had no idea what the teachers were on about, no idea at all, not for one single lesson. Not even for a bit of a lesson. I looked at the lads in my class and thought, 'If only you knew,' but they will never know and neither will anybody else. I don't think now that I ought to tell my wife everything that's happened to me—if I ever should get married. Perhaps it is one secret I should keep even from my wife, which is a pity really because I have always thought, right from being a little kid, that if you found somebody to marry, you should share everything, good and bad. Anyway, we'll have to see about that when the time comes.

Another thing I started to do was to wash myself more often and more carefully. I even bought a toothbrush and got a lot of *slaum* from my family when they found out. Mam said it was a stupid thing to do and I was getting above myself. Dad said it proved what he thought all along; I was a poof. I couldn't help laughing at that and, wow, did I get a belting.

On the Saturday I got there very early, but I didn't go straight to the spot. I wanted to see how she got there, if she walked or drove a car. And what sort of car. It had occurred to me that I hadn't noticed how she spoke. That might have been because of what we were doing together, but more likely, it was because she spoke like us and I wouldn't have noticed a difference because there wasn't one. If she walked to the wood then perhaps she lived not far away; if she drove, well, she could live anywhere. It was just curiosity on my part. I wanted to know a bit more about her.

The lane running alongside the wood had various parking places where walkers parked their cars before walking in the wood. But people only walked on the edge. I had never known anybody go right into the wood except the three people and me.

I knew I could get to the hut before she did if I saw her coming down the road, whether she was driving or walking. There was a good spot to watch from on the edge of the wood, and from there I could see every car and walker. I was wondering if she wasn't coming when an Audi saloon came and drove right to the back of the little pull in. It parked behind a four-by-four that had been there since I arrived and she got out. I set off for the hut so as to beat her to it, and I'd got my breath back when she came into the clearing. I was hiding and waited until she called, 'Hello, anyone in?' she asked and knocked on the door. She didn't open it, she looked round as if she knew I was still outside.

When I came out of the bracken she smiled and nodded.

'That's a very good idea, to hide until you know I'm alone. You can never tell who's around and we must not be seen together, you do know that, don't you, my young prince?'

And that was it. I was her young prince and she was a woman without a name. I never called her anything and it didn't seem at all strange at the time.

That third meeting was better than the second, and that's how it went on for months. Each time was even more exciting than the last with her doing things, and asking me to do things, I never would have imagined.

Some weeks after, I thought to notice if she was wearing a wedding ring, and she wasn't, though there was a mark on her third finger where one could have been. She had impressed on me that it was important not to ask questions about each other. 'I could be sent to prison because of your age, and how would you feel if you knew I was in a horrid place like a prison?'

When she said this I promised on my deathbed that I would never ever tell anybody, and all I wanted was to see her as often as possible and do the things we did.

Things never go on the way you want them to though, do they? Never. Something always happens to spoil things.

My mam didn't have a paper, she said newspapers were a waste of money and it was only occasionally that I got to see a local paper.

Sometimes I would read a bit on the front page of the *Guardian* when I was sent into Miss Barton's room.

When I was in there one day, not long ago, waiting to be reprimanded for missing so much school, I saw a photo on the paper's front page and it was the man. I was a hundred per cent sure it was him. It was the man who had been left in the hut. The one who had come to the hut with the woman and the other man. I was trying to read the piece when Miss Barton came in and she could see I was flustered.

'What a story. Have you read it? she asked.

I said no, but it was very difficult to control my anxiety and she moved the paper into her desk drawer before starting on to me.

She did tell me off, but Miss Barton was gentle when she spoke about my going missing. 'If only you could find someone who you could trust enough to talk to,' she said, and not for the first time.

Then she asked if I knew the man in the photo. 'I thought, when I came into the room, that you showed signs of interest in the story,' she said. 'Perhaps that's what you need, a confidant. A lot of teachers have had training enabling them to help people in all kinds of difficulty.'

I just sat quiet and didn't respond. We both sat in the silence for a little while and then Miss Barton whispered, 'You can go now.'

When I looked at her face I could see the same expression that I saw on the face of the woman who I had been seeing at the hut over the past several months and, seeing that, I didn't want to stand up. I sat there looking into her eyes.

'I wish I could help you, Tommy,' she said, in that same whisper, and I had to force myself up from the chair.

Before I had reached the door she said, 'Why don't you take the newspaper and, if you are free tonight, you can return it to my home. That is my address written on there.'

She was opening the drawer as she spoke, and looking down I could see the top of her head. There was a line of dark hair where it parted and I realised Miss Barton was not a natural blonde. I knew that because my Mam's hair had that same line, but grey and not brown. My nameless woman's hair was natural, black, and brittle down there.

I took the paper and waited until I got home to read the article with the man's photo.

They were seeking a woman who had conspired with her husband to defraud and blackmail the man in the photo, following the discovery of his decomposed body hidden in the woods near Cowswell. It went on, 'It is believed that the man responsible has left the country, but that his wife, whose passport had been confiscated for another offence, was still at large and believed to be somewhere in the Midlands.'

I did go round to return the paper to Miss Barton that evening. She was obviously expecting me and had a little tray with some cakes and biscuits ready. I sat where she said, in a chair opposite her, and when she had poured the coffee and sat down, I could see up her skirt. It was difficult for me to look away, and when I looked up at her face she smiled, and I knew she wanted me to look. My heart was pounding so much I thought she might be able to hear it. I daren't trust my hand to lift my mug of coffee.

She asked me why I had been interested in the newspaper.

I was ready for the question. 'It was this bit here about the actress and the bishop.' On the same page, down from the picture of the dead man, there was a story about a famous actress who had actually married a bishop.

Miss Barton laughed with me and it was the very first time I had shared a joke with an adult. In fact, it was probably the very first joke I had shared with anyone in my life. She had moved to the side of me when I looked at the paper and I could smell her perfume and feel her hair touching my face. She must have been able to smell my breath and I was glad I'd bought the toothbrush.

We went upstairs and were there for the rest of the evening.

When I had to go home she said I should keep the paper as a souvenir of a very special occasion in my life. I knew it was best to leave her thinking it was my first time, and she knew without it being said that I could keep a secret. Miss Barton knew that because of the hiding, and although I still do that sometimes, I don't need do it so often. Nobody could even begin to guess where I am a lot of the time now though, except for Miss Barton, of course, and everybody else just takes it for granted that I'm hiding again.

Blimey look at the clock, I'd better be off before the others get back. School finished five minutes ago and I don't want to keep the teacher waiting.

DO NOT RAGE AGAINST THE DYING

I hated these stairs when I was a kid.

Bed time, I hated that. The uncomfortable bed and rough blankets. Nobody would believe you today, would they? Young kids sleeping between blankets with no sheets, but that's how it was for us.

Dick never minded as much as I did. He had a skin like a bloody rhinoceros and could sleep through owt. The shouting and the crying, and the other noises, he never heard them. I did and it wasn't my imagination either, my sisters could prove that. It went on regular. Don heard it and he got in trouble for mentioning it. All he said was something like, 'That noise from their room kept me awake last night,' and he got a good hiding. Just for that.

There's still no carpet on the stairs, yet none of them creak.

That's how he managed to surprise us when we were talking and pretending to play. He could burst into the bedroom with his belt off and start thrashing before we knew he was there. He would pull the blankets off as we tried to cover our skinny bodies and belt our bare flesh. We never had pyjamas.

I think it was a game for him, part of the violence that filled his life. Cruelty was his hobby. Cruelty to the animals and to us, that must have been his major enjoyment, and see where it's got him.

What he said was law and he could do whatever he wanted. Nobody would want to argue with him. He never had proper friends, nobody could ever get close to him. He was nothing but a brutal bully, and we were all frightened of him.

That's why I've come back. To see him helpless.

There's a light at the top of the stairs now. There didn't used to be. There was no bulb in the bedroom either, just another empty fitting. We had a broken bed with a flock mattress, and in winter, coats would be on the blankets to help us keep warm. Three lads, little kids, with the girls in another room where the noises came from. He would sometimes take his belt to them, but mostly to us.

I was the only one afraid of the dark. Terrified while the others slept, keeping watch for the bogeyman. They never knew how much they owed me for keeping them safe. Because I stayed awake, burglars and bogeymen didn't come to haunt us.

Just him. I could hear him creeping about in the night; his shuffling feet and heavy breathing gave him away.

The banister has been tightened up. That'd be Dick, he was always handy, even as a kid. Not like me and Don. I suppose that's why he got most encouragement, because he could do things. He would encourage him as we grew up. He took Dick ferreting and learned him how to do things with animals.

I don't think he taught Dick the bad things though. Not the very bad things. Why did he tell me about it, the bad things? Was it because he knew that I was more frightened than the others, or was it because he wanted to impress me for some reason? God knows, I don't.

This morning, when I decided I would come, I'd thought about bursting in and shouting to surprise him when I got up to his bedroom, but, no, this is not the time for that sort of hank. I'll compose myself and try to look normal. Well, not normal. When your Dad is dying, normal is sad and unhappy, and I'm not going to try that. If I could do that I would be in the running for a bloody Oscar.

Is this muck on the stairs the same muck that was there years ago when we were kids? I read somewhere that if you don't clean up, your house gets to a point where it doesn't get any dirtier. I got a bloody good hiding for writing my name in the dust on the sideboard once. It was there for ages and ages, reminding me of how daft I had been to do it. I could have said it wasn't me, but then we would all have got a really big beating, and I didn't dislike my brothers and sisters that much. Not that they liked me. It doesn't matter now, does it?

Interesting that he lived such a long time after Mam died. Him who never lifted a finger to do anything, not even when she was really ill. Don said he propped Mam up to the sink to do the dinner and wash up.

Don told me, at Mam's funeral, that he had hastened her end by not doing anything to help in the house and yet, somehow, he had managed to live on in his filth for all these years. I only came to see him once. Once was enough with all his slaum and anger. He was still a frightening figure, even when he was crippled and old and frail. His eyes were still afire with the same fury that frightened me when I was little, and I knew then that I was never going to be able to get my own back for all the stuff he did to me.

It doesn't matter now.

I used to hide away mentally in books at the library, and hide physically as well. I had hiding places everywhere.

The door to what was our bedroom is closed. I'm tempted to open it and look inside, but a bit frightened to do that. I don't know what I'm frightened of now though; it's a strange thing, fear. It's almost like a disease that you can never cure. You learn to live with it, but you can't always shake it off.

I think I can hear him snoring. I'll stand on the top step and wait a bit just to gather myself.

Interesting that the front door was open when I got here, not that there is anything worth stealing, there never was. I could go in and smother him now and nobody would know, would they? It's tempting.

I'll go in here where we slept as kids. Just to see. It might get something out of my system.

It's still there, the broken bed, but the blankets have gone. I wouldn't let our dog sleep on them. I often say, 'Our dog sleeps on better bedding than we did as kids,' and folk laugh. They think I'm joking.

I don't think they make beds like this now. Coiled springs stretched across an iron frame and a lot of them broke or missing. The flock mattress is gone and the smell. That was awful sometimes. Pisspot's gone as well. We had to use that as a lavatory because we weren't allowed to go down to the one outside. It wasn't always emptied either. It stopped smelling after a time, until you pissed again and then it smelt worse than ever.

We stunk. As kids we did. I remember the remarks made by others and not always by kids. Grown ups sometimes.

'Just look at the state of that child,' I heard one woman say. 'He must have gone to bed like that.'

Of course we did.

Well, I'd better go and have look at him

Just look at him lying there. He's turning over, he might be waking up, I can hear him snorting.

'Hey up, there. How you feeling?'

God he looks terrible. Cheekbones almost sticking out of his narrow face make him look like a puppet. A badly made puppet.

'It's Tommy, Tom, come to see you. How are you?'

He's recognised me, I'm sure. If he's as well as he looks he's not very well at all.

'How you feeling?'

Is he humming or trying to speak? Like the rest of us he hummed, but not in a musical way. I heard him whistle a few times.

'Are you trying to say something?'

I don't know what 'ung ung' means. Just look at the state of him.

'Has the nurse been in? The door was left wide open?'

I thought I'd mention that to worry him.

'When I got here the front door was wide open, anybody could have got in. You could have been robbed, burgled, murdered in your bed.'

He's staring at me now as if he's struggling to make out what I'm saying.

God, the state of this bed.

'I'd put some clean sheets on for you but I don't know where they are. I'll tell the nurse if she comes while I'm here.'

If I did know where the bedding was I wouldn't do anything about it. What did he ever do for me? Bogger all, outside of the slaum and good hidings.

You could almost plant seeds in the muck on that dressing table. I'm going to write my name. There, Tommy Goodwin.

'Just wrote my name in the dust, 'Tommy Goodwin' it says here. I got a bloody good hiding for doing that when I was little, didn't I? Can you remember?'

He's still looking at me with that same expression, but his eyes have changed. He knows who I am, he used to look at me like that when I was a kid.

'My name, I have left my name on your furniture. Me, I did it.'

He's just staring. 'What are you thinking now, eh?'

I wonder if he can think. He never did much of that, thinking.

Mam didn't either, he saw to that. She never stood a chance, not with him bullying her all the time. I once made her smile and he came in and said, 'What you bloody grinning at, you soft bitch.' Then, for no reason, he said, 'You'll laugh the other side of your face in a minute,' and she scuttled off into the kitchen to have a cry. He liked that, making folk cry.

He's 'ung ung-ing' again. He can only do it soft. Trying to lick his lips now. I bet he wants a drink.

'Want a drink do you?'

A little nod. He can hardly move.

'You haven't got one here.'

I'm tempted to let him thirst on.

'We couldn't have a drink when we were in bed could we? Can you remember? I was so dry when I was a little kid I drank some water out of a hot water bottle that I saw in your bedroom. I was parched on a very hot night, so it must have been in that rubber bottle for months because you only had the hot water bottle in the winter. It must have been very old water, and it tasted very strongly of the rubber. Would you like a drink of rubber water?'

Ooh, the malice in his eyes. Ha ha, I think I've got him going now.

'Can you not remember? I'm here to remind you now. That must be why I've come. I was wondering why I'd come, and now I know. It's to remind you. You know, share a few memories.'

'Why did you tell me about the killing? You told me how you used to torture the animals for fun, and how to kill them in different ways. Why did you have to tell a little lad about that sort of thing? Was it because you were lonely and wanted to share things with somebody? Tell somebody who was so frightened of you that they would never dare to tell anybody else about it?'

His eyes are really blazing now.

'And the sport. Can you remember telling me about the sport with the dogs? With the dogs and the other animals? The little cockerels you would set onto each other?'

I will get him a drink.

'No, I'm not going. I'm getting you a drink from the kitchen. Don't go away, ha ha. Wait here and don't move.'

'Can you remember that? Outside the pub? "Wait here and don't move," you used to say and we waited, and waited, and waited, and waited. You bastard.'

This would happen time and time again. We would get so cold because often we weren't wearing warm clothes. They didn't seem to notice, Mam and Dad, and we'd stand shivering and people going in and out would look at us with a sad look, and know they daren't say anything to them inside where they were warm. Then, after a couple of hours, he'd come out with a bag of crisps and a bottle of something that tasted of piss. Eh, I could do that now, couldn't I? I could piss in a mug and bring him that to drink.

He's closed his eyes. He's having some trouble breathing now, so I'd better nudge him to say I'm fetching his—ah, he's watching me again.

'I'll get you a drink. Be back in two hours.'

Dear God, the state of this kitchen, it's worse than I remember it and it was bad when we were kids. Ooh, just look at this mug. It's caked up with muck. Well, I'm not going to wash it, that's not what I'm here for, washing bloody pots. Oh no.

The old wireless is still there, but I don't want to switch it on, the whole thing is greased up. You can hardly see through to the figures on the dial, and look at this spoon. It must have had gravy salt on it or something. Well, when the kettle boils, I'll use it to put the sugar in his tea. I'm not going to have one and I don't really know why I'm making him tea. Habit, I suppose. You go into a kitchen and you make a cup of tea. Well, most folk do, don't they? He never did though. I can't remember him making a cup of tea, or washing a pot, or wiping one either. She had to do everything. And yes, she even wiped his arse before she died.

Tea in the caddy? Yes. Nothing has changed has it? But why should it? He wouldn't have tea bags, or anything else that might have made life a little bit easier for her.

When I bought her the washing machine ten years ago, he asked me if I was going to pay the bloody 'lectric bill. He would have had her ponching the clothes in the tub till she died.

This milk's not very fresh, but it'll stir in.

I'll resist the temptation to spit in it. What good would that sort of thing do?

'Here it is then, a nice cup of tea for my dad. It's a bit hot for you to drink; we don't want you scalding yourself now, do we?'

He's looking up at me with such a malicious expression. I've half a mind to pour it all over him.

Is my mind filled with all the horrible things that he always said and did? Is that where all this is from, this anger and hate? Am I reflecting back to him what he sowed in me for all those years? Shall I ask him now, here, before he dies? What would be the point? He never thought about anything. He wouldn't know, would he?

Does he know what I am thinking?

'I'll put it here to cool and help you up in a bit so you can have a drink.'

This cupboard at the side of the bed is filthy. The sheets look as if they've been on the bed for years. Probably have. His face is grimy with dirt in every wrinkle. Under his mouth, alongside of his nose, across his forehead.

'Shall I get a cloth and wipe your face? That's a good idea, isn't it?'

God, this bloody kitchen. I think some of the smell comes from the drains. I bet there's never been a drop of disinfectant put down the sink for years.

I'd better boil the kettle for some hot water. Whatever made me suggest this, wiping his face? He never wiped mine, not even when we were kids. He didn't. Never touched us lads, except with his belt. I think I must be going soft, doing this.

What a surprise, there's no soap. Never mind, I'll use this bit of washing-up liquid. Bloody hell, it must have been here for years. The bottle top is clagged up.

The only cloth I can find might have been used to wipe pots at some time in its life, but it'll do. He's in no position to be fussy. Not that he ever was. Fussy, I mean. He would spit into the fire, because of the pit dust that got onto his lungs. Sometimes he would miss and it would go on the oven top and sizzle. Mam had to wipe it up when he missed altogether and it was her that wiped up the mess from his animals. He fed the dogs on scraps and anything to hand. Sometimes what he gave them was unsuitable for dogs and it would make them sick, but it never troubled him. Nothing troubled him at all. He didn't just ignore crying and pleading, he enjoyed the misery he caused and went on to create more.

Mam learned not to cry. Not even when he broke her bones and she had to go to hospital. She would just whimper a bit and look so miserable, and that made him even madder.

Everything would set him off. Everything you did or didn't do, and not just when he was drunk. When he hadn't been drinking he was just as bad, worse really because he could devise ways to hurt you more. Clever ways, devious ways that I don't want to remember. But you never really forget.

'Here it is. When did you last wash your face? It's terrible. No need to look at me like that, I'm here to help you. Lift your chin up, come on. Yes. Bloody hell, your neck's even worse than your face. Look, I'd better fetch a bowl; this cloth isn't going to do it. Wait here. Ha ha. And don't move. Don't *move*.'

Where the hell am I going to find a bowl among this mess? Kitchen? It's more like a garden shed. I wonder if Mam ever wanted a proper kitchen with a stainless steel sink and a proper cooker. She never said and now I'll never know.

Ah, here's a bucket, that'll do. I wonder what's been in it, what it's been used for. Something's set on the bottom.

Oh, God, it's some bits of fur.

Here's a little bowl that's had a plant in at some time. The dirt in it is covered with mould. If I empty in into the bucket and rinse it out under the tap. No, no, I've just had a thought: I'll tip it out the door.

That's a bogger, I can't get the back door open. It's stuck fast and the window over the sink as well. They can't have been opened for years. Sod it, I'll scrape it out onto the floor. Nobody will see it amongst all this crap.

'Perhaps the tea is cool enough to drink now. I've put two sugars in and stirred it, come on, I'll help you up.'

Oh, the stench when he moved, I wonder if he's shit the bed. Anyway, that's not my problem.

'There's no need to clutch the bedclothes to you like that. Do you want me to hold the mug? Okay. Take your time, you're not going anywhere.'

He's not got his teeth in. I expect the carer's moved them so he doesn't choke. If I find them I could put them in for him before I go. Just imagine if I did and he choked to death. 'Man killed by act of kindness.' That would be the headline in the local rag.

'Had enough? I can fetch another, it's no trouble.'

He's still got the malignant stare.

'Do you want some more tea? No? Right, I'll do a better job on your face and neck then. I've got some warm water in this bowl. I'm going to try to prop you up. Help me, lean forward a bit. That's better, I'll shove the pillow behind your back. Most people have pillow cases on these you know.'

He ignored that. Ha, who knows what he's thinking?

'This is called a bed bath, it's what the carer is supposed to do regular. When does the nurse come? She's supposed to check on your condition. You are bloody filthy. I'll give them a ring when I get home. This is not right, not right at all.

'Let go of the sheet so I can get to the front. No, let it go, I need to wipe your chest.

'There's a bit of water on the blanket, but it's not much and you do look better with a clean face. Better than you did. You're ready to receive company now.'

He obviously doesn't want me to do his front, so bogger it. I'd better not try to empty this water out the window. I'm sure they have never been opened for years.

'Do you want to use the commode before anybody comes? Does anybody come to see you?'

Gosh, he's answered, shaking his head.

'Nobody?'

Another shake.

'Just the carer then?'

Now he's sneering. The mouth is down in a way that I recognise from the old days.

'She doesn't seem to do much.'

Now he's really angry.

'Should I take it up with the authorities, would you want me to do that?'

He's shaking his head, I think He actually looks frightened. I've never seen him look frightened before. Never.

'Is she a problem, the carer?'

He's breathing heavy now. I think I've struck a nerve somehow with this talk of reporting the woman who comes in.

'What's going on then, is there something you want to tell me?'

Oh, that brought a quick refusal.

'Are you sure? You seem to be bothered by me mentioning it?'

His eyes have closed and he's still breathing heavy. This is not the time to ask him about the mess in the bucket. Before I go I want him to confirm that my guess about that is right. He did have two cats.

'Do you feel better, you know, after being cleaned up?'

No answer. He's pretending to be asleep.

'Can you remember that time you took me rabbiting? Once was enough for me. Lying down in wet ditches to hide from the farmer, you seemed to think that was fun. It wasn't fun for a nine-year-old. And all that walking. Miles and miles over rough ground, and for what? You said it was sport. Sport, you called it. And the way you dispatched the rabbits. If you could kill like that, why did you want to do what you did the other times?'

He's still, not moving, but I know he can hear what I'm saying.

'You thought it would make a man of me, showing me what you did. Fun, you said, a bit of fun. Treating living creatures like that. Is your mind still as warped, or do you feel sorry for all the misery that you caused? You can pretend all you like you can't hear me, but I know you can.'

He's turned to look at me. It's still a bit frightening, even though he can hardly move.

'Are you sorry now, now you are near the end of your life?'

Stony stare, holding back the truth, just like always.

'You do know you are dying, don't you? I didn't come to gloat, just to see what happens to someone who, at the end of his life, caused such pain and unhappiness. You were my dad. You never acted like the dads I read about in books. Yes, you can sneer. You never liked books and you never liked me reading them either. Is that why Mam never read a book in all her life, because you never allowed her to? Were you afraid of what we might learn, was that it? I used to hide in the library to read, and when I got carried away with a good story and got home a bit late for tea, you would be angry and send me to bed hungry.'

That always upset Mam, then she would shout at me as well, out of fear for what might happen to her.

'What a way to live. Did you think that was how normal people carried on, how ordinary people lived in ordinary homes? *Did you?*'

I expect I'll never know now. He's not going to tell me now, is he? And he wouldn't if he could.

I loved the books, any books, all books. I accidentally picked up one called *And Quiet Flows the Don* and read it without knowing it was a classic. Then went on to read *Virgin Soil Upturned*, I think it was. He thought reading was for oddballs.

'Weren't you ever tempted to read a book? What about books on cruelty? There's lots of books about that. I bet you would have enjoyed *Never Come Morning*, I think Nelson Algren wrote that, or *Last Exit to Brooklyn*. They were all about cruelty, your subject. You would have got a university degree in that subject, you would. Practical and theory. A masters, a masters degree you would have got. No problem. But you wouldn't have got much in the dad stakes. I wonder if you were the worst of all dads.'

'Did you not like being a dad? Was that it? Did I ruin your aspirations? Ah, perhaps that's it. My arrival spoiled your chances of a higher, more cultured *laife*. Some people who get educated talk like that. "Ai've hed a very gud laife."'

What am I on about? This is brave talk to a dying man who can hardly get his breath. 'You thought I was odd, didn't you? Because of the books and me starting to wash and try to keep tidy. The dentist laughed when I told him about the toothbrush. Remember? We never had a toothbrush when we were kids and when I started my paper round and bought one out of my spending money, you thought it was proof I was "one of them". You bigoted swine.

'You always had a best suit, but what did Mam have? *Bogger* all. I know you can hear me getting this off my chest, and I expect you don't like what I'm saying. But it's taken me a long time to get round to say it, hasn't it?'

Oh, he's turned round to look at me. Isn't that odd? It's a look of pity. I'd swear that he's got a look of pity on his face.

'Are you feeling sorry?'

The sneer's back.

'Are you feeling sorry for me, is that it?'

Bloody hell, he's nodding a bit. 'Sorry for *me*, you are actually feeling *sorry* for me?'

I think his eyes are laughing and his face is contorted.

'You're bloody laughing at me, you bastard. You are lying here in this filthy bed, in this filthy house, dying. And you are feeling sorry for me?'

He's watching me like a hawk. Watching my lips and now my eyes.

'Were you always laughing at me?'

I never knew that. I never saw him, could never tell that he was laughing at me. I always knew he hated me, but I didn't know he was laughing at me. But why not? He laughed when he tortured the animals. Not a proper laugh, like when you think something's funny, but a hard kind of laugh. A horrible sound.

'I don't feel sorry for you. I don't feel sorry that you had a horrible life and had the accident. I was glad. When Mam said you'd been kept in hospital, I hoped it would be forever. I hoped you would die. Did you know that? I was praying you would die and not come home again.'

There's the contempt. That's a look I recognise, and I expect I deserve it, saying this. But it's true. I wished many times he was dead. Time and again I would hope and pray that he would be buried down the pit and never come back home. But he always did, in some shape or other. Like a living ghost he was. He still is.

Now he's actually dozing. I expect it's knowing he can still get to me that's made him happy enough to sleep. He's having trouble breathing. That'll be from the accident on the coal face. He broke some ribs and they punctured his lungs. He was in a right mess and it was touch and go for several days. I didn't go to see him in the hospital, I was fourteen years old and managed to get out of it. I was gutted when Mam said he was on the turn and would get better. I think that was the moment I stopped believing there was a God. I wonder how she felt. Apart from the little muted cry, nobody could ever tell how she felt. If she did feel anything, Mam was bloody good at hiding it.

What am I waiting for? I ought to go now before he wakes up. No, he's watching me now.

'You could have a little telly up here, you know, would you like that? You never liked the wireless, especially the music. When I heard Mario Lanza singing I thought that was the most moving sound I ever heard. 'On with the Motley', he sang. You scoffed at that. We didn't need any bloody motley in our house. We needed no clowns here, did we? What a circus though. What with you being drunk and violent, and Mam pretending it was all normal, and what was happening with the girls, and Don and Dick learning how to cope with it all, and me never managing to do that. I couldn't could I? I couldn't cope. I just hid.

'I could never do anything right, could I? Whatever I did was wrong, and you bloody loved it, having a prat like me to kick around. All the time you were telling me, time and again, that I'd never be any good, not at anything. Not while I ever had a hole in my arse. That's what you told me, right from when I was a little kid. Just a child. And you drilling it into me that I'd never be any good. What a bloody start to life. And I grew up believing it. No matter what I did, or managed to achieve, I could never take the credit for it. Lucky, I was, it must have been luck because I was no bloody good, no good at anything, was I?

'And I never managed to do enough to make you eat your words. Do you know something? I must have been well into my twenties before I learned not to care, before I thought, "What does it matter? What is his opinion worth? A cruel, ignorant bully."

'When I landed the job looking after Littleford's pigs you were full of contempt, even when I got the silver at the Royal. That was when I realised I cared more about them animals than I did about my own family.'

Hello, somebody's come in; I heard the door go. That sounds like a man's voice, more than one. I expect it's the carer. I don't want to see them, and I don't want them to see me. I'll go into the other room to listen, and then I'll have a better idea what does or doesn't get done.

It sounds as if they've had a drink, shouting up to say they're here and he's trying to speak to me as I leave.

I don't want to get involved with them, bloody carers and social workers. They'll have me taking responsibility for him if I'm not careful and I've no intention of doing that. I'll wait in here till they've gone.

Good God, what's that? I wonder what they're doing to him. He's kicking up a fuss, but there's not a lot he can do.

You can almost hear folk breathing through these walls. I could as a kid. Mostly Mam's muffled crying and the other noises. When I was very little I heard some awful sounds in the night and . . . There it is again. It must be hurting, whatever they're doing. I expect they are trying to sort him out, but it's odd, I can hear them laughing.

'Can't stop,' one says. Bloody Nora, they've only just got here and they're going, laughing all the way down the stairs. I'll give him a minute and go back in.

'What's that smell? I thought I could smell smoke. Do they smoke while working? How professional is that?'

Perhaps they smoke to hide some of the smell, I don't expect they go into many houses that stink as bad as this.

'Is something burning? That's not cigarette smoke, it's more like scorching. They haven't dropped some fag ash on the bed have they?'

He's looking pretty bad and it seems like he's been crying.

'Did they ask who cleaned you up?'

He's not responding now. He seems to be in shock or something, just lying there clutching the blanket to his chest.

'Shall I make you another drink? Tea?'

They've left the bloody door open, I wonder if it was them as done it before. How many times a day do they come? I'll ask him when I've made this tea. It's not right that they should leave the door wide open, anybody could walk in. Mind you, a burglar would be hard put to make anything from here. There's not a single stick worth a bean and the bits that are here are all mired in grime.

'Here it is then, tea. I've stirred the sugar in. Are you alright? You look terrible. Does it make you feel bad when they come to see to you? I didn't know you had male nurses, but I suppose it's better that you do. They weren't here long were they, what exactly do they do?'

I think he's crying, making the strange noises while he's clutching the blanket to his body.

'Do they give you an injection, is that it? Does it hurt?'

I can't make head nor tail of this He's obviously very distressed.

'They shouldn't leave you in this state, I'm certain. I'll ring the office about it. Have you got a number where I can speak to somebody?'

I think he's losing it. There's tears running down his face and his nose is running.

'I'll wipe your face. Just lie still while I get the cloth again.'

I'll soon get used to going up and down these bloody stairs, the number of times I've done it this afternoon.

What on earth was that bang? 'Hello up there, have you fell out of bed? Hang on, I'll come back.'

My God. 'Don't scrabble about on the floor, I'm here now. I'll help you up. Just try to hang onto my arm and . . . What the hell is this? What's happened here? Your chest . . . Let go of the blanket. Were you trying to get to the commode? Right, let's get you there, but let go of the blanket. You'll fall over it. Look, I've seen your chest, so let the blanket go onto the floor and I'll straighten the bed while you do what you need to do. Good. I'm going to turn you onto the seat now, then I'll leave you sitting there while I fetch another drink. Don't try to move till I get back. It's too easy to break something at your age. I'll not be long.'

I'm not sure who to ring. His chest is a terrible mess. There's something radically wrong here. Why didn't somebody dress the wound, a nurse or one of the carers? Why haven't they arranged a cleaner or some help? Surely to God even he shouldn't be left like that. If I ring 999 for an ambulance will it get the carers in trouble? And what if it does? They can't be doing their job right to leave an old man like this. He's in a right mess. Bogger it, I'll ring.

'Hello, yes, we need an ambulance, please, for my dad. Kettle Street, number forty-nine. I found him in a right mess. There's something wrong with his chest. I'm not sure, I think he's in his early eighties, they don't have birthdays in this house. Yes, I'll wait, but how long will it be?'

I'd better get his tea. I'll not tell him I've sent for the ambulance.

'Come on, let's get you back in the bed. I've brought another drink. Do you have any medicine or pills or something to take when you feel badly?'

He's bloody awkward to shift, 'Try to move your feet to one side. Yes, I'm being careful to avoid touching your chest, but we've got to get you back into bed. You might well have visitors on the way.'

Bloody Nora, that's the door. 'Just sit on the side of the bed while I see who it is.'

'That was quick. He's upstairs, I've just got him off the commode and seen his chest. Come and look.'

'What a good job I cleaned your face, you wouldn't want the man to see the mess you were in would you? They're going to put something on your chest while we ride in the ambulance. He's getting it now, but they have to know who did it. Those two men, were they nurses or carers?'

'No, I didn't think so. Don't worry, the paramedics have notified the police. How often did they call in, was it more than twice a day? Do you know who they are? Are they local?'

'He's not asleep you know, just pretending. Yes, of course I'll make a statement to the police, I want these bastards caught. I don't think they were kids. Well no, I just caught a glimpse of them leaving as I got there, I didn't see what they were like, but I could hear them speak and they were grown-ups, youths.'

Jesus, I've got to be careful what I say. I don't want the authorities to think I did anything to him, and I don't want anybody to know that I was hiding while them men did it.

'You read about these things in the paper, it's as if they aren't real life, but I expect you see it all the time.'

He's listening to every word, I'm sure of it.

'That was quick then. Here we are, Dad'

He looked up when I called Him that. The ambulance man noticed.

'Shall I stay with him and wait? Is that allowed? Can I get him a drink from the machine? He likes his tea.'

The man says he's to have nothing till the doctor sees him. I'll stay and find out what they are going to do with him. His chest is such a mess, but that hasn't all been done today. I wonder why they would do something like that. Does he owe money, or is it somebody he's done wrong to in the past and they're getting their own back?

He can't talk, but he's not missing a bloody thing. He looked at me then as if he knows what I'm thinking.

'We've got to wait here till they find a bed for you.'

He doesn't seem bothered, not about any of it.

'Here's a bobby. Yes, this is him here. He's not asleep. Dad, Dad, it's the police to ask you questions, and he's going to take your photo. I expect now it's all digital, you don't need a proper photographer. Oh, sorry. Did you hear that, Dad? He is a trained photographer. Yes, it's his chest. You've got to let them do it, Dad. For evidence.'

'All right, if that's what you want constable. I've got to go and wait in the waiting room, they want to speak to you on your own. He can't say much, you know, constable, but he can make noises. You'll know if he says yes or no. I'll wait to find out what's going to happen. See you soon. Oh, there's a woman policeman here now to sort you out. It looks like you're in good hands.'

I hope they get the truth about what happened, I'm a bit worried that he might make out it was me. He's hated me all my life and it's true I wasn't much of a son to him. I ignored him after Mam died. He could pretend it was me that's been doing that to him. There's no proof. No proof either way. That I did or didn't, that's what bothers me.

How long are they going to be? I've been here the best part of an hour, and left sitting here like a bloody lettuce waiting for salt. What happens to the new magazines? Surely somebody must leave fresh ones now and then. *Car*, and *Woman and Home*, and one copy of *National Geographic*. What a bloody choice.

'I am, yes. What's happening to my Dad? Well if they are keeping him in, that's obviously the best thing, he's got nobody to look after him.

What, now, with you? No, I came in the ambulance. Alright then, but I can't tell you anymore than I told the ambulance men and the constable.'

It's my first ride in a police car. 'Which station are we going to? Right.'

Waiting and waiting again. But at least I'm not surrounded with badly folk like in the hospital and it's a comfortable chair. The bobby says they are waiting for news from the doctor and they want a statement. But why have I got to wait all this time, the bloody day'll all be gone if they don't get a move on.

'Yes, officer, of course I'll make a statement, but I haven't seen much of him over this last five years or so. Why should I need a solicitor?'

'Dead? Well I'm sorry, but I had nothing to do with those cigarette burns. I could smell a scorching smell, that's why I said burns.'

'Charging? Me? No, I said, I told you I had nothing to do with it. It was two men who'd been to see him before I did. They must have done it. I don't know who they were. I can't believe this is happening. Yes, of course, but I don't have a solicitor. Yes, I'd better wait.'

God, I'd love to light up, but that's the last thing I dare do, I've been charged with aggravated something or other and I've got to stay here till it's sorted out.

Yes, you old bastard, I bet you're having a laugh now.

I'd better be careful; I think that bobby saw my lips move.

TOM'S A SINGER

Prison stinks. Sometimes I think I can still smell it on my skin and on my clothes—what few I came out with. Strange though, I was getting used to it, being inside. They say it's the first time you hear the cell door slam, that's the worst. But they are wrong. Very wrong. It's when you wake up after a few minutes sleep on your first night and think you're dreaming and then you find you aren't. That's when the shock hits you. Several of them inside agreed with me on that, but perhaps it's different when you know you're innocent. A lot say they've been fitted up, but even if that's true, it doesn't mean they're innocent. That's why they got done, framed. The Bill know that the man in question is guilty and they don't want him to escape justice, so they do their duty, as they see it, and fit him up.

I wasn't framed. They were genuinely wrong and that was my bad luck. It was my good luck when somebody grassed up the two that did it, done my Dad. Mind you, that poor sod who spoke up was in a mess when the police rescued her from them two psychopaths. She was covered in cigarette burns and in a worse state than Dad, but she was younger and survived to let on about what had happened. She was bloody lucky that a neighbour smelled smoke and called the fire brigade. More than one fireman was sick when they burst their way in. The young woman was tied to a bed and had been for days. Gagged and drugged and tortured. Just for fun. For sport.

It'll be a very long time before the pair of them get out to do more damage. I don't think they should ever be let out because they can't be right in the head. A sympathetic policeman told me that during the court case both of them pleaded they were under the influence of drugs, and he said that has become the norm now—to try and get some pity from the judge. It didn't wash this time though, and they are going to serve a very long sentence.

Mr Littleford gave me my job back, taking care of his pigs. Alice, the prize sow, remembered me, she didn't half make a fuss, and there's talk of me getting compensation. When I heard this I was thinking I might start a little business with a few pigs of my own, but Peggy, who was waiting at the gate when I came out of prison, said I shouldn't do anything until we come back from holiday. What a holiday we had, and then she talked me out of the idea.

She never seemed to smell the prison on me and still laughs at me bathing and showering so often.

'What about how you smell when you finish work with them pigs?' she asked once.

Funny, but I never thought I smelled bad, working with them. I probably didn't, it's just that she wanted me to find another job so we could get married, one with more money. But I loved my life with those animals, and they liked me as well. You should have seen them react when I got there in the morning, especially Alice. She was a beauty and should have got the gold in the Royal.

I swore I'd never go down the pit.

'I'd look bloody well, giving up a job like I've got,' I said. But I knew Peg was right about the money, it was crap really.

When I came out I kept thinking how I could make some cash on the side, in my spare time. While I was in prison I did a bit of singing with a group. They were in for shifting drugs and could they play. Bloody hell it was music as good as I've ever heard, and they liked my voice. They were a big encouragement and said I should take it up semi-pro. You can make some good money doing the working men's clubs round here now. It's not like the few pound they used to pay years ago, it's twenty, thirty pound now for just the one night. Peg laughed at me when I said I wouldn't mind giving it a try, 'Wouldn't you be better off at the pit like other men?' she said, and she wouldn't let it drop.

I don't remember saying we would get married. She implied I had and I could only think it was when I was drunk one night. Most women don't like their man drinking, but Peg seems to be the opposite to most women and not just over the drink. That's what made being inside worse. I'd got used to having her every night and sometimes in the afternoon as well. She'd come up to the farm looking for me and it was just for that. Bloody hell, I'd never heard of such a woman. It was as if she couldn't do without it. She could hardly go all day and very often didn't. It was as if she was addicted. Peg was the opposite to Janey.

Jane wasn't like that. We knew each other from when we were kids, but she went off to college to learn to be a teacher. Peg thinks she's stuck up, but I know different. Jane is more sensitive and more sensible, and bloody clever with it. I do sometimes wonder what I'm doing with Peg instead of Jane, but then Peg starts her tricks and I fall for it again. What man wouldn't?

She kept on pressing to get married and when I said, 'I can't see why we should, because what would we do that we don't do now?' She said, 'Just you wait and see.' I sometimes wonder where she gets all her ideas from.

I thought it was best if I just concentrated on getting back into the job and bringing on Alice. If she was as easy to bring on as Peg we would have had the gold in the bag, but to win, this lovely animal had to peak at exactly the right time. She had to shine on the day.

The gaffer kept saying how much was riding on Alice and I was beginning to get a bit nervous because of all the pressure. But what a pig! A great breed, the Landrace. She walked well and stood well, like a beautiful statue, but you can never tell for certain what will happen on the day. Perhaps that's why I was seeing so much of Peg, to take my mind off the worry.

I wasn't bitter about the wrongful conviction. I think that's because of the relief I still feel every day since being cleared. Bloody hell, I could have been in there for years instead of a few months They don't let you go if you don't own up to doing it, even if you're innocent. Is that so they can believe they've been right all the time? Anyway, I'm out now and getting on with my life.

They let me out for Dad's funeral, hardly anybody turned up. Dick came, but there was no sign of our elder brother, I expect Don was celebrating somewhere. He hated Dad even more than I did.

I tried to explain to Dick that while I was inside for what I didn't do to him I could hear Dad laughing.

'When did you ever hear Dad laugh?' he asked, and he had a point there.

Although I'm not bitter about that, I am bitter about not getting the Gold though. Everybody there knew it was a twist and some said so to me after the judging. Alice was turned out perfect and behaved like that as well. Everything bloody perfect, and only got the silver. I could have cried and did when I was on my own after.

Peg didn't go to the show. I was a bit disappointed at that, but when I saw Jane, who was home for a while, I felt better.

It was no surprise when Littleford told me he was selling up. He'd dropped enough hints about what would happen if Alice didn't get the gold, but I was really upset when I thought about Alice going. I would love to have bought her for myself.

My old mate, Boscoe, said I should go ahead and borrow from the bank.

'Start up on your own, Tommy,' he said. Then he asked if I knew Jane was back.

I said, 'Yes, I still fancy her, but how could a pig man marry a teacher? I'd be marrying above myself, wouldn't I?'

His wife said, 'You shouldn't let that stop you, all men do.' And I'm not sure she was joking.

The compensation came through for the time I'd been inside and I was daft enough to tell Peg. The first thing she said was, 'It's not enough, not for what you went through. Get a lawyer. They are doing you down with a sum like that.'

When I said I thought it was fair, she lost her rag with me, 'That's your biggest fault, Tommy,' she said, 'letting folk shit on you all the time. What do you think Mr Littleford was doing and what did your Dad do all them years? I'll tell you this. When we are married I won't sit back and watch folk do that to you, my love. You'll have me to stand up for you then.'

Sitting there quiet with her raving on, I thought I might well have second thoughts about getting married to her. Little did I know what the future held for me and little did I know when I was chatting to Jane at the Royal Show that events had moved on and Peg had a surprise up her sleeve.

Only it wasn't up her sleeve, was it?

It all came together. Missing out on the gold, losing my job with the pigs, and the news from Peg that she was pregnant.

At first I tried to convince her that we could make a go of a smallholding with Alice, who was up for sale, and a few fowls and rabbits. She was scathing. 'What do you think this is?' she said, patting her belly. 'A bloody litter? Get real, you prat, and get off to see that under-manager at Shonkey pit'

I dreaded the thought of working underground after being out in the fresh air.

A week or so later, Peg bought two tickets for us to go on a coach outing to Doncaster races and on the way back we stopped off for a drink at a big pub where they did music. The artist hadn't turned up. Customers were going on the stage to do a turn when I recognised the man accompanying them on the organ. It was Terry who had played while I sang in prison. When he saw me he almost fell off his stool, but I didn't let on I'd seen him before.

'What key do you do "Rosie" in?' I asked and he was trying not to laugh.

'Well you start and I'll follow,' he said.

He knew full well where to start and we were away.

'Cracklin' Rosie make me smile, We're gonna rock until there ain't no more to go . . .'

It brought the house down and they were shouting 'More, more.' The landlord came over as quick as he could move and asked if I'd stay on the stage and do a spot. I asked him how much. While he was thinking and trying to guess, Terry leant over and whispered something to him.

'If you're prepared to stay through till closing time and do three spots, about twenty minutes or so, then I'll pay twenty,' the landlord said. I caught sight of Terry's face. 'Thirty,' I said and he nodded. As he was leaving the stage, the landlord turned and said to Terry, 'If it turns out he's rubbish, play loud and drown him out.'

What a night. We went through all the stuff we'd done inside and then some more. The audience wouldn't let me finish when time was called and the landlord had to turn the mic off to get us to pack up. It was one of the best nights of my life.

Peg got to like it after a while, me being up there on the stage, but she kept an eye on the women. Funny, women who wouldn't have given me the time of day before, suddenly wanted to know me, and I mean, *know* me.

I kept putting off starting at the pit, thinking I would get discovered, but it didn't happen. Looking back, who was going to come anywhere near Cowswell to look for talent?

I tried a few jobs as Peg's belly swelled, but there wasn't money in them, not enough to meet her needs, so that's how I got to go down Shonkey.

It was the worse thing I ever did in my life. I hated it. Every single shift. I could do the job, I was strong enough with all that lifting on the farm, but being down there on the coal-face, so far away from the land and the light, I thought it would drive me mad at times. Some of the chaps were alright, and I never let on that I preferred the company of my pigs, but it was bloody hard. It was a struggle to keep going to work day after day, but I did it. Mainly for him, I suppose, the lad.

Peg wanted everything at once. We only had a little house, two-up and two-down, but she had to have a bedroom suite. It nearly filled the bloody bedroom, but she had to have one so we had it on the never-never. You know, on tick, and it seems you are paying forever with the interest they put on.

The more I earned, the faster she spent it, and if I dared to question her she would make such a scene that I gave up. I gave up everything except the singing. I think that kept me sane.

It was nice watching the lad grow though, and working shifts I could spend some time with him. She said, 'No more.' And that was it. He wasn't going to have a brother or a sister.

The sex wore off anyway, as I understand it does for all women, and then I realised how little we had in common. I wanted the lad to learn; she couldn't have cared less. I wanted to do what I could to get him into the local grammar school; she went on about how much the bloody uniform would cost.

'And that's only the beginning,' she said, 'What about the cost of the things they do, going abroad and sports and things. They don't come for nothing, you know.'

I said I would do overtime and she railed on, 'You do bloody overtime now and we can hardly manage.'

I looked at her, thinking of her trips with the 'ladies' as they were called. She never missed one, and while she was away, her mother had to come over to stay. She was always a nasty piece of work.

'It's nice my Peg can have some space for herself, isn't it?' she would say. She was said trying to provoke me, but I never took the bait.

Sometimes I would call in the Golden Bull to have a pint, but I wasn't really a drinking man. I enjoyed listening to the stories and thought about writing some of them down, but I didn't. I imagined what Peg would say if she found out I had taken up writing. The slaum would pour out of her mouth non-stop. It was nice to have a laugh though and a lot of what was said, tales and quips and things, were funny. Then I would go home to her mother, old bloody misery guts.

I did a lot of overtime, double shifts when I could. What a way to spend your youth, working your life away down there in the dark. What's more unnatural than that?

I don't know how accidental it was, that meeting with Janey. I remember it was early on in the day and I looked round and she was there, right at the side of me. I used to go to the site of the old tip.

It hadn't been a tip for years, it was from the days when everybody burned coal. In the late spring and early summer the entire surface was covered in weeds waist high, and then almost completely bare for the rest of the year. Skylarks laid eggs on the ground, and in the hedge that surrounded it, all manner of birds nested. It was said to contain poisons in parts so it was almost always deserted, except for the odd dog or cat, or sometimes kids being daring. It was a place where I went to watch and get away from Peg and her mother. There wasn't much to watch mostly, but it was quiet and, leaning on an old gate, I could dream. I still did that and I'd been working down that bloody hole for fifteen years. I didn't dream any more that I would be discovered as a singer, I knew that wasn't going to happen. I was singing in the local pubs and clubs, and I'd accepted that entertaining the locals was as far as I would get.

Dreaming about what could have been, I knew I'd turned into a bloody 'coulda'. At that time I believed there was only two sorts of people who lived in Cowswell: 'gunnas' and 'couldas'. Gunnas were men under forty who weren't happy with their way of life and talked all the time about how they were going to change things.

'I'm gunna emigrate, or join the army, or buy a chip shop, or take a course in plumbing, get a smallholding, or go north, or south, or . . .' But they never did. And then one day they became couldas.

'I coulda emigrated with our Harry, coulda joined the army, coulda bought a chip shop, coulda, coulda, coulda.

But it was too late. A life they detested seemed somehow to have them trapped, and I knew, staring across the tip one day, that it had trapped me too.

Then there she was, Janey. 'How long you been there?' I asked, not knowing what else to say.

It took a little time before she answered, 'I've been here watching you. You were miles away, Tommy.'

I could have cried at the sound of that voice. I've always loved music, but no music, symphony or lark, ever sounded like her voice on that morning.

I was too full up to risk saying much and she could tell. She looked lovely. Her eyes were as blue as the sky above, only bluer. I felt like I was melting away, and when she smiled I had to look away for fear of bursting into tears. All the rough life and the swearing and dirt and grime of my living just fell away, and her being there renewed everything. I felt like a young lad who'd been badly and had suddenly got better, and I wanted to reach out and touch her. Not in that way, but just her arm or something, so as to make sure she was real.

And do you know what? I could tell she knew exactly what I was feeling. Isn't that odd? Two people separated for fifteen years or so and a magic was there holding us together. I wanted to stay there forever. For all of the rest of my life, looking at her and listening to what she was saying, even though I couldn't tell what that was. I was watching her lips move and listening, but I couldn't hear the words, just sounds, until I heard her say she was back and was going to start teaching at the school.

'Here, at the comp?' I could hear myself ask, and it seemed as if my voice came from miles away.

She nodded and my heart soared, up there with the skylark that was near the top of its flight.

'You used to hide among the weeds on there when you were little, Tommy. Remember?'

I nodded, 'And you were the only one dared to come and find me and ask me to come out.' I was choking. She looked away so as not to embarrass me.

'I'm sorry about your Dad and the problem his death caused. When I heard about it I was angry. I knew how much hurting he had caused you while he was alive and then, even after he died, it seemed he could still continue to do so. And I can hardly imagine the disappointment you must have felt when Littleford sold the herd. It was what you did, you knew everything there was to know about your stock, Tommy.'

Her voice was clear and steady and full of meaning, every word, like it had always been. I shrugged, as if it wasn't important, trying to appear manly, 'We didn't win the gold at the Royal, and that was it.'

'From what I heard, you should have done. I was tempted to write. It must have seemed like the end of the world. Well, it was the end of your world, Tommy. I still can't imagine you down the pit.'

The sadness in her words was not a reproof, it was a genuine pity and I daren't answer.

'I heard you've got a son.' There was no reproach or anything like that in her voice.

I nodded. I was trying to make the words so as to speak and I wanted to ask if she was married, but I daren't. I couldn't tell how long that silence lasted. She stood quiet, alongside me against the gate and watched the weeds waving. If I'd been a poet or something I might have thought they were waving sideways saying 'be careful', as if they knew what was happening between us at the gate. Thinking about it after, I thought perhaps all of nature knew and was warning us because the same wind that was moving across the field was also travelling across the sky, which was suddenly getting darker to one side. We still had the sun on the old tip, but to our right we could see low black clouds. I didn't speak; it was sensible Janey who spoke.

'We'd better take cover, Tommy, where you used to hide,' she said.

I stood without moving, hardly breathing, and stunned to think that she could remember that we hid together once. It was only once, and it was more than thirty years before.

'I wonder if it's still there,' she said.

My chest was pounding and I felt numb.

'Your hiding place, do you think it's still there?'

I knew it was because I still used it when it came on to rain and I didn't want to go home.

We walked close, but not touching, along the side of the tip to where a railway bank had once carried a track. There, in the side of the banking, workmen had made a hole, boarded it up, and put a wooden door in place to cover the entrance. I always thought it had been made by the men who laid the rail track through the countryside. It was somewhere to shelter from the weather and where they could eat at snap time. Over the years the doorway had been covered by growth, branches from elders had leant over it and shrubs had grown up in front of it, so nobody knew it was there. It was a good hiding place.

I was shaking when we went in. Jane was surprised to see a mat on the floor and a little folding chair.

'So you come here often, Tommy?'

It wasn't a question. She knew, without me saying, that this was a refuge for me.

'And you can't even offer me a cup of tea.'

She was smiling and we were very close. I shook my head, 'Sorry.'

'It's alright, really it is. It's just nice to see you again and to be together after all this time.'

She was holding my hand as she finished speaking and that was when I dared to put my arms round her and pressed us tight together. I could hear her breathing right close to my ear and I knew then, by that sound, what was going to happen.

It would have been better if we could have moved outside when we had finished, but the rain had come so we were stuck in there. We couldn't escape from what had happened.

Right from the beginning when we were in primary, Janey was more grown up than I was, even though we were the same age. I didn't know what to say. I wasn't going to say I was sorry, because I wasn't. But I knew what had happened, wonderful as it was, must have been wrong. It wasn't my first time, playing away, but it had never meant anything before. What had happened between us, Jane and me, on that day, meant a lot. More than I could say or think.

It was as if she could read my mind, because she took hold of me and hugged me and made me feel as if it wasn't wrong after all. Perhaps I'd got the feeling mistaken, perhaps what I was feeling wasn't guilt or regret for what had happened. Perhaps what had seized me inside was the realisation that here was the love of my life, and I had messed my life up, and it was too late to put it right. And I wasn't going to be able to be with this lovely woman who had always known me better than I knew myself.

I remembered how I got through the bad times down there on the coal face. I would tell myself that I was alright. For this second, I was alright, and that's what I did. I held her and let myself wallow in that second and the next and the next and the next and . . . I don't know how long we held each other. Neither of us wanted it to end, and when she made as if to move, I held her tight while I said what I'd been waiting to say.

'Janey, I love you. Please say we can see each other again.'

And she hugged me tight and said yes very quietly against my face. I felt her lips moving as she said it, 'Yes.'

'You'd better wait here and give me a start back, Tommy,' she said, but I was panicking.

'When though, when can I see you again, Jane?'

'You work shifts, that much I know, so what shift are you on next week?'

The thought of not seeing her till next week dropped my heart down into my boots. 'What about tomorrow?' I asked.

She nodded, 'Same time then, same place, by the gate.'

I stayed where I was and watched her straighten her skirt and run her fingers through her hair. I was wishing they were my fingers when she smiled and reached over for one last kiss. Then she slid out through the covering that hid the door.

While I waited, I stood and cried. I was loaded down with a feeling of helplessness. The only anger I could muster was toward myself. I had taken the coward's way out, the easy way, whenever I had been faced with a challenge and this was the result. I had always had a heart more full of hate than love. Mostly hate toward him, my dad, but to others as well. Standing there, I suddenly realised how much I hated myself and how much I loved Jane, and how I was filled with the need for her, this lovely woman. I just stood crying and feeling physically sick.

It was some time before I went home, I'd just got enough time to grab something to eat before I set off to work, and then a strange thing happened. I was walking as if I was treading on air. Me, going to Shonkey pit as if I hadn't a care in the world. It came over me all at once, as if a great big, black, heavy wet blanket had been lifted off me.

A blanket I had carried to smother my mind and my soul for bloody years, and I was free of it. I was in love with a wonderful woman who loved me.

The next few hours did drag a bit, but down there time passes with the shovelling and the setting of props and I was more careful to do that than I had ever been before. This shift I didn't want the roof to cave in on me. Not with what I'd got to look forward to now.

Peg was not concerned with my coming and going, not as long as I was ready for work when time demanded. That was a good thing. I wanted to see Jane as often as I could and we did meet up a lot, if not often enough. Jane was busy and had a lot of work to do in and out of school hours, but we did manage to get some time together, and it was marvellous. I think I can speak for us both when I think about how it was. Bloody marvellous.

When I sang locally Jane would come with some friends and nobody seemed to notice how I sang to her. I didn't have to be all that careful about Peg noticing anything was going on anyway. She didn't care about me at all, not as long as the money was coming in, and now that was a blessing.

I lived for the times when I was with Jane. It wasn't always physical. Sometimes we would sit and talk and she listened to the dreams I carried and she never sneered at them. She never criticised me, or tried to get me, to change anything, although sometimes I could tell she would sooner have us be together, properly together. But never once did she suggest I should leave Peg. Not once.

For the very first time my life seemed to have a purpose, even going to the pit, as if it was part of something to be alive for. Well I did have something to live for, and in my head, I was daring to make plans. Secret plans that I didn't even mention to Jane. At first I couldn't tell if they were plans or dreams, but as the weeks went by I could tell the difference. It was timing that was important, and with timing a dream can be turned into a plan.

I didn't try to hide the magazines from Peg and she sneered and laughed.

'*Smallholders Monthly*, and what is in there to get you excited? A photo of a pig? Is that what you need to get you going now? You bloody fool. If you think I'm going into the wilds of bloody Lincolnshire to live in a shack, miles from anywhere, you've got another think coming.'

I never responded and that always makes her more angry. She'd slam the door on her way out to go round to sit with one of her drinking pals and moan about 'his behaviour' as she puts it. It doesn't bother me. All the time I think about Jane. I can see our lad feels sorry for me sometimes, but I always pass it off and tell him it'll not always be dark at six. He doesn't understand, but perhaps he will when the time comes, I hope so. I am a bit concerned about him. He is well under the thumb of his mam and she'll do anything to use him. I'm bloody sure of that.

It won't be dark at six then, by God it won't. It'll be sunshine every day. I'm making plans and I've already asked the lad to do some figures. He's bloody good at maths and, although I don't let on, I think he might have a suspicion that it's all more than just another exercise. I've got to have some figures to go to the bank with. When I told Jane I was making plans for the day when I could get out of the pit, she was so pleased for me. I haven't spelt out to her where she fits in yet and I won't, not until the time is right. The lad has got another year to go before his important exams, and then, well, that's it.

Funny, but I've no doubt about Jane coming with me, even before I ask. When we talk she's always concerned about me. About my welfare. She does worry about me working underground and that makes me feel good, I don't think anybody's ever worried about me before, never. Not even my mam. These years with Peg have set me wondering about all sorts of things. When his mam's around, the lad never shows affection and only the slightest interest in what me and him do. But when she's not there, he's a different person.

I wonder what my mam would have been like without that bloody bully there. He was no sort of dad to me, and perhaps he wouldn't allow her to be a proper mam.

Anyway, I have started to put all that behind me now, thanks to Janey. I have explained to her that I'll make big changes when the lad's done his exams. She thought that was very considerate.

'No more than I would expect from you, my love,' she said. There's times when she makes me feel proud. Not something I've ever felt, ever before in all my life.

On my way to the pit I would block out for a while where I was going. Sometimes I was walking in the Cotswolds. Through the little villages and the beautiful countryside that I'd seen in magazines. Jane had encouraged me to read Zola's novel *Masterpiece* and after that I walked through the streets of Paris, but hills and open landscapes were best. I could picture so clearly the home that was waiting for Jane and me somewhere. Now that was easy because, years ago, when I was little, about nine or ten, I'd gone to a place right out in the wilds of Lincolnshire to see how people lived on a smallholding. It was little more than a wooden shed, but a family lived there, a man and his wife and two little girls. I never forgot that day because it was the first time I'd seen two girls who were blond-haired and clean. The little house was spotlessly clean inside and the girls as well. I knew they were looking at the dirt on my legs, and that made me feel more self conscious than ever. Then the youngest, who would have been about six years old, whispered to her sister, 'Look at his neck,' and I knew what they had seen. There was always a ring round my neck where the dirt washed to when I rinsed my face under the tap. I was torn between wanting to get away from the place and wanting to stay and live like them. To get clean and live in a clean, tidy house. And the eldest looked at me in such a kind way, as if she was sorry for this scruffy, young lad who was going red-faced in front of her. She was about my age, the eldest, and she was so pretty. My heart melted inside me, but I didn't kid myself, no girl like that would ever want anything to do with me. And I found out years later that the peaceful rural scene wasn't what it seemed. It wasn't the idyllic little life that I had imagined it to be at all. A few years after, the truth came out when the man was in court for organising dogfights and badger baiting. Another dream gone.

Sometimes, as a little kid, I felt I had nothing to cling on to except my friendship with Jane, and I was always frightened to push that.

I wonder if it was when I heard the child mention my dirty neck? Something set me back. I was frightened of everything and everybody.

Not now though. Not now I've got Jane. I can walk to the pit with my head up knowing it won't be like this for the rest of my life.

I wonder if that little shed-house is still there. I wouldn't know where to find it and dad's dead, so he can't help, but Alf Littleford's still alive. We went there in his trap, pulled by that trotting horse. I think I'll go round and ask him after I've worked this shift. He's an old man now, but he's still all there.

It's good to make plans. It almost makes this rotten life worth while. If I worked down here for fifty years, I'd never get used to it. It's not for me, and the thought of getting out of it and being with Jane, and having a smallholding with my own pigs, well that's what keeps me going now.

'Creaking a bit, is it?' One of the lads coming off the night shift says the coalface is a bit unstable, but it doesn't bother me. It's always been a good seam, Deep Soft, not very high, but safe, well, most of the time. No face has ever been completely safe.

Here we are. When we come down the pit it takes over an hour to get to the coal face where we're working and it's not easy walking either. I still find myself thinking though as I walk.

It would be nice if we could find that place in Lincolnshire. I remember there was a wood nearby. I could see it from the house, and one of the girls there asked me if I was frightened of being in woods. I told her no and had to stop myself asking if there were some good hiding places there.

I don't need to hide now, well only to have some time with Janey, but that's not hiding away like I did before.

The roof is straining a bit, but I'll make bloody sure I put the props up sharpish. I'm risking nothing, not with the life I've got ahead of me and—

Oh God! It's coming down, the roof. All the roof. Oh no . . . No . . . No!

TRAPPED

It's rough this, lying here in the dark hardly able to move. If I do, it might make things worse. Not that things could be much worse. It's a bogger, I don't know how long I've been here, pushed down into this blackness.

I can move my head to one side, but there's nothing to see. I seem to have lost my helmet with the lamp. A smell of dry dust though and that's a comfort, there's no water come in, just the bloody roof. I wonder how much came down, how far the fall stretches. If it's the whole coalface I've had it. Wonder what time it is. Wonder what bloody day it is. What's happened to the others?

Odd i'n't it? I must have been knocked out, that's why I can't remember what happened.

There was a bang, thunder, and the loudest most frightening noise in the world. Well, when you get it down, here it is. That's when the earth gets its own back on us for what we do to it. Tearing its guts out then using what we get to pollute the air. If that's not adding insult to injury, then what is?

There's a lot of interest in that sort of thing now, not like years ago. We didn't have all the chemicals and machines, not on the land that is. I miss being outside, always have, but I came down here when we couldn't afford a proper bedroom suite, that was it, to get some furniture for the house. Wouldn't take much, it was just a little house, two-up and two-down, make a bit of money, then get out.

I can clench my fingers, on both hands. What does that show? I haven't broke my back, that's a good thing, well it is if they get me out.

How long could a man stay like this before he dies, I wonder?

What a price to pay for bloody furniture and things. You never stop once you get started. After the house got sorted it was the car. All that bloody rotten interest we paid to borrow for a car then came the cost of running it. That meant more overtime, more time spent down here, double shifts. I must have been mad. But this, what's happened, was never going to happen, not to me, not like this.

Mind you, we aren't finished yet. They know I'm here, and if—when—they dig me out, well, I'm bloody finished at this game.

It was never right for me. I missed the stock, especially the pigs. Folks don't know how intelligent pigs are, brighter than most of the prats I've met down here.

My legs hurt, but that's a good thing, it shows I'm not paralysed.

Things are still now, nothing falling, no dust trickling, that's when you have to go and you can shift. Like a rocket on all fours. This time though we didn't get a chance. I think it's coming back . . . the big bang and not knowing which way to crawl because there'd been no sign. No cracking, no dust trickling, just a bang that deafened me. That was it, I remember now.

I remember Alice. Silver at the Royal Show, better Landrace than the winner. Best pig in show, but only got second. That was because Jackson had the name. He knew the gold was his before we paraded Alice, probably knew weeks before. It wasn't straight. What is?

Wish I could straighten my back a bit, just to lie flat. There's something under my shoulder, digging in. Bloody hell, I could kill a pint, a mug of tea wouldn't come amiss.

Oh God! Something's moved. If any more drops, I'm a goner. Jesus, oh Jesus! That was another stone moving.

Ah it could be them trying to get me out.

'Here! Here! I'm in here!'

Nothing, not a bloody sound now. It couldn't have been them. God, if any more roof falls in they'll have a job on. Where the hell are they?

Ought to be getting me out by now. They'll know I'm here though. Wonder how long it's been.

Have they told her? Ha, she'll be in a state if they have, bloody Nora, I can just imagine. She'll have the policies out, and her mam'll be round enjoying it. Press job, I expect. 'He was a fine man, good husband.' All that crap. They said that when Bushy got killed. 'Fine man, good husband.' Good husband bollocks. Never stopped knocking her about, but she got her own back then when she got the compo. New car, holidays 'to get over it.' She bloody hated him. It stopped her wanting to get married again, even if it didn't put her off men. She was popular then, by God, she was. Good at it an' all. I had some of that and enjoyed it. A lot of us did.

Will my Peg be like that? You never know. You think you do, but you don't.

Who'd a thought this would happen? Oh, I'm dry. I think it's that that kills you, no water. If I could get my hand up I might suck a bit of coal if I could find a piece. The way my luck's gone, I'd probably get a bit of stone. You can't suck that, it's not like coal. I suppose it's because it's never been alive.

I was alive once, when I was on the farm. I was always dead down here, a living death.

Ha, I remember that Monday morning dropping down in the cage. Everybody muttering, 'Roll on Friday.' It was only when Gordon said, 'Roll on death' that it struck home. That's what we were saying really. Just wishing our life away because we were in this dog hole. I must have been stupid.

My bloody back, I've got to try to move it somehow. . . That's a bit better. Can't move too much in fear of bringing some more roof down.

How long they going to be? Shall I try to stay awake? I'm boggered if I know what to do for the best.

I'm glad our lad didn't come down, I made sure of that. I'd sooner see him a tramp than be on this bloody hank. What a way to live. Ha, what a way to die now if they don't get me out. . .

Not a sound.

I can still move my hands though, that's a good sign, even if I can't move much else.

Jane said I'd got nice hands. We were friends from school days, she was sad when she heard that I'd left the farm to go down the pit.

'It's not my business, but you're not like them, it's not you, Tommy.'

Jane would have been better for me. This proves it. I should have married her, but she wasn't as forward as Peg. Peg knew how to wangle things, knew what she wanted and how to get it. When I got this job she didn't bother, just glad the money was coming in . . . and Peg never said I'd got nice hands. They're not nice now, but Jane still likes me to touch her. She's lovely, lovely to me anyway. Doesn't like me working down here. She understood, knew it was wrong. If I do get out, I ought to go off with her and perhaps this is the time to make decisions like that. One thing is certain, I shall not come down again, I'd sooner eat grass.

Ah, a noise. God, are they coming or not? How will they know I'm here if I haven't got a light on?

They'll know, cause they'll know. They're forced to know I'm here. Perhaps they think I'm dead. Well, they'll have to think again cause I'm not. Not yet, nowhere near, I can stick this out. Never let it be said that I was a bloody jibber.

I must have been asleep. God, I'm dry, I'd pay a tenner for a pint. We all shall if it keeps on going up. Oh God, ooh my back hurts. I'll have some lamp in the ambulance room before I set off home. I'll be going home soon when they get me out. It can't be long now. They must know I'm here. They must be trying to dig me out. It seems a long time though, a long time to be like this, like a bloody rat in a trap, worse.

I never liked going ratting. The others did though, cruel bastards. Enjoyed the killing, the blood and bits flying.

'Watch what my dog can do.'

Didn't like it. Just seemed wrong to get enjoyment from suffering, whatever was going through it. Now it's me, it's my turn. I'm going through it . . . Well, it's not that bad really; I can move my fingers and that's a good sign. I'm tired, it might be a good thing to sleep and just wait for them to get me out. They know I'm here.

Oh, bloody hell, I must have dropped off, I've been dreaming. This is not a dream though, wish it was and I could wake up in bed. I can still move my fingers and my toes in my boots, but the stone wedged over me stops me from turning. Wonder how big it is, wonder what's holding it off me. Whatever it is, I hope it stays put.

I was dreaming about you, Jane, not her, not her I'm supposed to think about. I should have left Peg and married you, I shouldn't have waited. Look what's bloody happened, oh God, what a price to pay for one mistake. If I had married you instead of Peg you'd never have let me come down here because you had different values, you were always different in lots of ways. Even though I was married you still loved me and waited and waited. You'll be waiting now, I know. I'm sorry, lass, I'm sorry to put you through this and if I do get out we'll bogger off, you and me. Sod 'em all. Daft i'nt it, what it takes to bring folks to their senses? Oh Jane!

Oh, my back, I'll try to shift a tiny bit. Perhaps if I move a fraction now and then it might be better.

Our lad knows about fractions, my God he does. In line for a university place if he sticks at it. This should help really, shouldn't it? He'll not want owt to do with this now, not that he ever did, but this'll be a clincher. Ha ha. If they don't get me out he'll probably come in for some compo if he plays his cards right, and if he does, I hope he don't let his mam get her hands on it. He's not that daft though, he knows his mam. He's a good lad, bloody clever, all there he is. Makes you wonder where his brains come from. He's mine though, spitting image even on them photos took when he was young. Folks would say, 'God, that's your lad, right enough.'

What sort of lad would we've had, Jane? Or perhaps a girl to look like you. If only, *if only* . . .Geordie Tom said they were the saddest words in the English language. But you didn't think I was soppy when I told you what life I wanted, when I talked about the books. You were always interested in things, a different sort of life, a smallholding. 'You know all about pigs,' you said. 'All there is to know, you know. How many get a silver at the Royal, and it should have been the gold—everybody knew that.' You were such an encouragement all the time.

If I concentrate on you now it might get me out of this alive, Jane. Oh Jane. Oh Janey. Janey, my love, please help me, help me to hang on.

Oh, there's a light, everything's lit up. Why can't I see owt? Am I blind? Who put the light on, Peg, is it you? What the bloody hell's going on, what's happened? Why can't I see? Has the clock gone off? Have I overlaid lass?

Ooh I've banged my head. Ouch ooh. What the hell's going on? It's dark, it's dark, black, oh, oh, oh . . .

I've been sleeping. Not out yet, ha ha, not out, no, not bloody out. Still trapped in this bloody hole. Wonder if I should say a prayer? What good would that do and what a time to turn religious. If God wants me out he'll know what to do. He'll not need me to tell him. Is he laughing? Wonder if Jane will remember that one about God, I'll bet she does. I remember. When I told her about getting enough money to buy a smallholding in Lincolnshire and all the figures our lad done to prove what was needed to make it pay, she smiled and said, 'If ever you want to make God laugh, tell him your plans.' Is he laughing now, I wonder?

What's the first thing to do when you get out, Tommy? This is a good idea, positive thinking, let's have a quiz.

Well, Tommy, what's the first thing you'll do when you get out?

We've had that question.

You didn't answer it.

Oh no, you're right, I didn't.

A pint; no, a bloody great mug of tea.

And who will you want to see first?

Jane and my lad, I don't want to see anybody else, I'll tell the lad me and Jane are going away together and we'll go. I think he already knows about us, he must do, the time I'm missing. Hope he understands, I think he will, he's a good lad. He must be worried about his dad, not knowing if I'm alive or dead.

Why don't they get me out? All this time and everything quiet, not a sound, nothing. Quiet as a grave. Bloody hell, don't think that, don't think that, Tommy, they know you're in here and they'll be digging now. Making it safe, testing for gas. If they can't get to me in time, gas would be a good option, that don't take long to kill you, you don't know you're gone. Mind you, there's no trace of it on this face. It was a good coal face this one, not very high, but high enough, and safe. Ha, that's a laugh, ha ha; safe, yes, isn't it just.

Think positive, Tommy. The smallholding, that's what I was thinking about, going off with Janey. Think about that, Tommy. Just a little house, two bedrooms, we'll not be having many visitors, just the lad I should think. He might help out a bit, with the pigs. His mam never succeeded in putting him off altogether, much as she tried. He can do the books for us lass, if you don't want to that is. You've got the brains to do whatever you want. Never knew what you saw in me, but we clicked and that was it. You done a daft thing falling for a prat like me, but we all do daft things sometimes, it's making it right when you realise, that's what counts. Well I'm going to make things right now, when I get out, you just see. You'll see, you'll see what I'm really made of. I'll be the man you thought I was. We'll show 'em all. Us happy, that's what counts.

If I dared just get one hand to feel up to my belt I might find the lamp cable and if it should still be fastened to the lamp, well. The battery is on my side and if the cable is still in one piece I might be able to get the light on if the bulb isn't broke. Ha ha, like that joke Body said. Two tramps and one said to the other, 'If I'd got an egg we could have egg and bacon, if you'd got some bacon.' He can tell 'em Body can, wonder if he's alright. How many got out? I hope there's enough to dig me out, but it's funny, I can't hear a thing, you'd a thought I could have heard something unless the fall stretches all along the face. Well if it does, I'm in for a long wait.

Got it! The cable's in my fingers and, aah, that's what digs in my back, it's the lamp. Ease it, ease it, Tommy, pull it down gentle, gentle, bit at a time. Ooh, here you are my beauty and here's the switch. Steady.

It's on, a light. Oh God, oh God. It's like being in a coffin. Oh God. Tommy, Tommy, Tommy, Tommy don't give in, don't panic! Put the light off and lie still. Use the light when you can hear them coming. You'll be alright. Think about what you'll do later when they get you out. First thing, a pint, second thing, another pint. That's more like it and it's easier to lie flat now that lamp's not digging in your back. You're doing alright, lad, you're doing alright, and if you keep your nerve you can make it, you'll see.

How many pigs would we want to start with, Jane? I suppose it depends on the compo. This getting buried could be the way out for us if they play fair—*if*. They don't always do that though, do they? When Uncle Jack got killed they didn't play fair, the bastards. They said it was so much per cent his fault so Auntie only got a little pension, hardly enough to pay the rent and she'd small children. Will we have children, Janey, it's not to late, is it? Wouldn't that be something, eh, a little lad with your brains, or a lass with your looks and brains. Bloody hell, one of each and happy ever after. And some bloody good pigs with one good enough to win that gold at the Royal. Can you imagine what it'll be like? A new life free from bother, just happy, you and me, happy together and . . .

Stay, stay, Janey, it'll not take long and you look so lovely. I'll love you again, Janey, stay lass, and it'll just take a few minutes, I'll rush back and make it up to you, you know that. I can't get this door open, why can't I push it and get back? Jane, Janey, please help me get back in, the door's fast, it's stuck, stuck.
    Oh, oh, oh . . .

Bloody Nora, I'd gone again. Come on, Tommy, hang on, they'll be here soon, it's just a matter of time, you're safe enough. Ha ha ha, safe right enough. Just one slab of rock held a few inches above my whole body, if it moves I'm dead, but if it doesn't they can get me out, prop it up and edge round it till they can pull me sideways. They'll do it and soon I'll bet. Not that I'm a betting man, well not for a long time. We had some fun though, me and Boscoe. Ha ha, we bloody did. It was me that worked it out, how to beat old Sutton. Well, he'd had enough off us over the years and it seemed a good scheme, backing winners. It was when they put a phone box down the New Road that I got the idea. Sutton would take the odd bet off us in the Golden Bull and even take one near the off if we were drinking together.

Boscoe would sit alongside Sutton looking through the paper and turn to the racing page, then say something like, 'Ooh bogger, I was going to back so and so in this race.' And Sutton would say, 'Well go on then, lad, I'll take it,' not knowing that I'd run from the phone with the winner and stood in the off licence where Boscoe could see my fingers giving him the number of the horse. We backed a few losers to keep it going, but when we'd won a fair bit Sutton stopped taking bets after time. Mardy bogger, typical bookie. Wonder what odds he'd lay on them getting me out now. They're a long time about it.

I am dry, gasping for a drink. When I told Bill, who worked with me on the farm, that I was coming down the pit he said I was mad. He came from Cleethorpes and he wouldn't go down the pit or out to sea fishing, but given the choice said, 'I'd choose the lesser of the two evils and that would be the sea because if the boat went down you were drowned in minutes, down the pit you could be buried for days on end to die slow.'

I bet he'll be thinking what he said now he's got the news of this bloody rotten hank. He must know, they'll all know. Nobody will cry more than Janey. Don't cry yet, lass. I'm going to stick it out for as long as it takes, I'm not done yet, they'll get me out and it is easier with that bloody lamp out of my back and I can switch it on when I hear them digging me out. Grateful for small mercies, that's me i'nt it, Janey? We'll show 'em, lass, we'll show 'em. I can move my feet a little bit so I'm not paralysed and my hands. There's not a lot wrong, ha ha, well not really when they get me out.

If I make plans, that'll be best, if I spend this time being definite and sorting my life out. Have I got one though? Is it just pretending? I've done a lot of that, pretending things are alright when they're not really. Do we all do that, I wonder; go through life pretending things are as we want, when they aren't at all, nowhere near sometimes. What have I enjoyed most? Well, that's easy. Being with you, Jane. The laughing and talking. You never minded me dreaming out loud, never said, 'Don't be bloody daft, you daft sod.' Like Peg did. I stopped telling Peg what I wanted because she could never see anything other than what was there in her face. I suppose she can't help that, that's how she is, but you're different, Janey, you can see what isn't there and understand when I sit and try to tell you what I want, even when sometimes I can't really describe it. All these years us mostly being at arm's length, yet always closer than anybody else. I know now what a bloody fool I've been, and if I'm given the chance, I can make it up, and I bloody will, you'll see lass.

I've never totally been a gunner or a coulder. You smiled when I told about them, you knew exactly what I'd seen. Peg didn't, she thought it was another load of bollocks like most things I said, but you knew, you understood. All the men down here under forty are gunners. They are all going to do something, 'I'm gunner buy a chip shop; go to Australia; get into the building trade; do a plumbing course.' All sorts of things, but they never do and then, when they are over forty it's, 'I coulder bought that chip shop on Highbury Vale for two hundred pound; I coulder gone to Australia with Uncle Ernie and made a fortune; I coulder gone off with Gyro and got into the building trade doing up old houses and retired at forty-five, I coulder . . .' But they hadn't done and time had gone and no bogger ever did anything, just kept coming down this bloody hole.

And now this. Oh, Janey, please get them to get me out. Please. I've been a bigger fool than any of them, at least I knew there was more to life than this and there will be if they get me out. Please, God, get them to get me out.

How many pigs do you reckon? If we get a good sow, perhaps two and then pay top money to get them in litter, we could try to breed another Alice, try to win that gold. We'd have the rest of the money to spend on the house. You'll make a lovely home, Janey, I know that, all clean and tidy, not fancy, bit plain, but everything lovely and clean. That's what I like.

It'll look lovely and nearly all your old furniture because it was good stuff. You never bought rubbish, wouldn't have owt to do with rubbish, 'cept me that is. I'm joking, lass, if I was rubbish you'd never have stuck by me all this time.

Come and give me a kiss, a cuddle, let's just cuddle. I'm getting cold. I'll make the fire up and we'll just sit and hold each other. This is nice lass, you're so lovely and I love you. You don't need to say owt, you let me go on and don't seem to mind. I'm tired, I'm tired, I'll have a little nap. Don't move, Janey, hold me and be here when I wake up. That's all I want.

Ouch. Oh God. Still here. How long they going to be? Come on, lads, get them shovels going. You must know I'm here. Bloody hell, somebody must be doing something to get me out.

I was dreaming again, about us, Janey, being together, the two of us. You don't have to give up the teaching, you know, I can manage the pigs and we'll not want to be out in the wilds. There'll be a school somewhere near and they'll be glad to set you on. With your reputation you'd get a job anywhere. You've always been well thought of, everybody knows that.

I'm going off again. Come on, Tommy, *listen*. You'll hear them soon. Wonder who'll be first. Perhaps it'll be the official rescue team, they'll have all the kit, stretcher, all the bloody lot. Well they needn't think I'm going to hang about, when I'm out of here I'm away. Bit of lamp to ease the back and I'm off home. Not that the back needs any lamp, but that's what you get now whether you need it or not. Since they put that heat lamp into the ambulance room it's never been out of use. 'Finest thing out,' the nurse says, regardless of what's the matter. Cures everything, bumps and bruises, bloody ingrowing toenails I'll bet. But I'll not hang about, Janey. You'll be there waiting, I'm sure you will, and I'll tell Peg what I've decided and we'll be off, together. No boggering about, get a few things and I'll come to your place and then we'll find that smallholding and away. That's us. Happy ever after and bollocks to them all.

Union can sort out the compo. Compensation runs into thousands nowadays, well, sometimes it does and if it does or does not, well sod it. I'll not be back down here again and I'll tell you this, I'll not do anything again that I don't believe in. It's no good and no good ever comes of it, it can't, not when it's wrong, You can't get right out of what's wrong. If only I'd have believed in that before. Well, I did really, but I didn't act on it, didn't live by it, that was the problem. Perhaps, for some of us, it takes something like this to bring us to our senses. Well I shall not need a second dose to make me do what's right, I know now . . .

A noise, listen, *listen*, Tommy. Is it them? Is it them, or is it some more roof coming down? Please, God, *please*. Let it be them. Oh please, please.

It's gone quiet again, I bet they're listening.

'Here, lads, here, I'm here! Come on, get through.'

The light, flash the light on and off. Don't look, just on and off.

'Aye up, lads, here, in here. I'm buried. Here, for God's sake, come through.'

Bloody hell, careful, careful, you'll have the bloody lot in. 'Hello? Hello!'

'I'm in here. Be careful for God's sake, I'm trapped under this stone. Can you hear me? Shout, shout you prats so I can tell what's happening.'

Oh God, nothing. It must have been some more roof coming in, that's me gone then. What a bloody way to go. I'm sorry, Janey.

More noise. Was that a voice? It was a sound. Am I imagining? It's a voice.

'Lads, here, I'm here. Be careful, I'm under this stone, I'm trapped.'

It is a voice, please don't let me be dreaming, please God.

'Yes, yes, in here lads. I'm here alive and well. Ha ha ha. I'm here. Come on, come on. Can you hear me? It's Tommy.'

'Yes, I can hear. Oh God. This way, be careful, I'm trapped. I'll flash my lamp. Can you see?'

Well who'd 'a' thought it? I can still hardly believe it. All that time and it was little more than twenty-four hours. Mind, I was one of the lucky ones, three killed they said, and some injured bad.

I was always lucky, 'cept for marrying Peg and going down the pit. Anyway, it's behind me now, now I can start to live. This is like heaven, being here in hospital, clean sheets and fresh air and light. Light, yes, that's the thing that matters. Unless you've known total absence of light, you don't know what darkness is.

This is lovely, everything bright and clean, gallons of tea. Bloody heaven. I slept like a log but that might have been the injection. To explore, she said, the nurse. They are very kind. But I want to get home soon and get on with my life. Celebrity now though, picture in the paper and fuss, loads of fuss. I can do without it. I've said nothing to Peg yet about my plans, but I'm going to go through with it. Not that I've had a chance to say owt to Jane, she hasn't been yet. Well, she wouldn't, with all the fuss. She'll wait till it's quietened down then she'll come, she'll come, then I'll tell her. Then I'll tell the lad. He was here this morning. Bloody upset, his mother was grim, but he couldn't stop crying, couldn't speak, just kept gripping my hand as if he was frit to let go. He cried more when I told him I was all right and it was all over bar the shouting. And his mam sat there, grim as death. Ha ha, but I'm not dead, not this time, this is where I start to live. I'll bloody show 'em.

Come on, Janey, come and see me, we've got a lot to talk about, a lot to sort out. I'm still tired mind, tired, tired out.

Oh God, oh God. It's dark again get me out, get. Oh. Oh.

Tea, lovely hot tea. Bloody hell, when I dropped off I was back down there again, but no more, I'll not be going down that dog hole again, never again. Out in the light for me. New life, new wife, new everything. They don't answer when I ask how long before I can be out and about, they talk about tests. Well bogger the tests, if they don't come up with something soon I'm discharging myself. Have to be careful though because of the compo, don't want to risk that. Me and Jane will need that, that'll fund our new life. Happy ever after life, that's what we're in for, lass, when this is sorted. I'll just have to be patient.

You didn't stop long when you visited, Jane, couldn't hold the lie. Like the lad, cared too much, that's why. Peg could, she could always put on a face, never found that hard to do. And the staff, all that looking away, they knew all the time, knew I was boggered.

The coal board will pay to have the house altered so I can get about and they said I could get a special car to drive with my hands. I've still got my hands, Jane, it was the hands that you liked. The rest of me's no bloody use and I'll not impose that on you. No, I'm going to have to let go of that dream. This is it for me, sitting and looking. I shall get some reading done now, ha ha. Spend the rest of my life reading and trying not to dream too much. There's nobody else to blame, but I am sorry, Janey.

The nurse passes a box of paper hankies when I cry, but none of them know what I'm crying for. They don't know about the smallholding and the pigs, just me and you lass, but we know now it can't happen. God, that's the hardest thing, not because I'm crippled, its the fact that we can't be together. I didn't have to say and you didn't either, you knew. You knew I would never come to you as damaged goods, I couldn't do that.

No, let Peg get saddled with this. She'll make a meal out of it, her and her mam. Bloody martyrs that's how they see their roll. And dip your bread in, that's what they think. Well, they've got another think coming. Ha ha. It'll be interesting when they find out what I've told the solicitor. I hope it'll be a long time before I'm dead and they read the will. There's cash for you, Janey, my love and for the lad when he's grown up.

Sometimes what I'm thinking makes my lips move and the staff look at me a bit strange, but I'm not bothered, they don't know. You'll know, Janey, when you come to see me and I can get to sit outside in the summer sun with you there. I'm going to tell you all about it so you know how much I love you. If we are going to be together it'll have to be in that next world you believe in and you'll have to get me a ticket into there.

I can hardly speak to Peg and I'm glad they're going to make a bedroom downstairs. I can't bear the thought of seeing that bloody rotten bedroom suite ever again.

THE VERY BIG EVENT

See, this is the trick. Being a bit conspicuous. It's no good trying to be invisible because you can't manage that. And anyway, for me to succeed I need to be noticed. Not too much in the way, or prominent. Just so that some will notice I was here, and afterwards those people will say, 'Oh God, I remember seeing that man sitting there.'

For years and years when I was little I tried to hide and I did everything I could trying to be invisible. When I got older I realised what the hiding was about. I was getting away from the world and all its cruelty. Now it's not just about me, but all the millions of other folk who get treated bad in this life.

Dad was always hiding I suppose, but he would hide in the drink, in the pub, and when he was at home, he was a real sadist. He treated us with total contempt. We were all frightened of him, and yet when I was little I would try and treat him like a normal dad. I would try to tell him about what I'd read in a book, or ask him a question about something I'd thought of. Why on earth I kept on doing that, when all it did was to get him going and make him lose his temper, I just do not know. More often than not it got me another good hiding. Ha ha, a beating I mean. That's what I would get before I ran off to hide, a bloody good hiding. And then my brothers and sisters would shout at me for getting him into a temper.

There was another bonus I got from hiding when I was a lad. But nobody knows about that, well only the two women involved. Thinking about it, I was unbelievably lucky in a way. The fantastic things that happened with them was some sort of pay-off for the miserable life I led. I ran away from everything and everybody except those two women and then, years later when I was grown up, I ran away from making the right decision when I had the chance to make a life for myself with the one person who loved me for myself. For who and what I was. A pig man. I'd have money on it, that if I'd have married Jane instead of Peg, I would never have gone down the bloody pit, even when the gaffer decided there wasn't enough money in pigs and sold up and I was out of work.

With her brains she would have arranged the finance and we could have taken over the herd and made enough to get us through till things got better. And they did get better, like I said they would. Bloody Norah, we'd have probably been the first to the line when organic got going. We were organic. I wouldn't ever have my animals eat stuff like other folk did. No, they would have had natural food like tater peelings and—— Oh, what's the use?

When the accident happened and I was trapped down there, on the coalface, I forced myself to think about a new day. A new dawn for us, Janey. Now? It's all gone, except for the grandsons, that is. Yes, they do act bloody daft at times, and the youngest, he gets mixed up in a bit of bother now and then, but it's never serious. Well, not very serious.

Would I be here doing this now, Jane, if I'd not had the accident? Would we really have made a life together when we could have done and lived happy ever after? I don't know, and nobody will ever know the answers to these sort of questions now will they? What did Geordie Tom used to say? '"If only" are the saddest words in the English language.'

Still, it's no use bothering about that now. I'm here to make a statement and that's what I intend to do.

I've got to get the timing right and I think I've got that worked out. Well, I should have, it's taken me a lifetime to get to this point and while I sit waiting I've got plenty of time to think. To go over the facts and frustrations that got me here to do what I'm going to do. And

I am going to do it, that much is certain. I haven't been coming here pretending to watch the trains for nothing. I've established a presence here over many months. Big part of the plan that. The plan for the very big event. Soon the waiting will be over.

'Oops, sorry, am I in the way?'

Chap caught the edge of his bag against my wheelchair. He reassures me I'm not in the way here and I know I am. Just a little bit. Just enough to be noticed. And I'm going to be here a few more hours so that loads of people can see me before the event. And I'm in exactly the right spot here.

I have often wondered if this all began at the pictures. The Saturday morning kid's show. The tuppenny rush.

I must have been no more than six when I realised that I was on my own. That I was the only kid there wanting the Red Indians to win. I suppose I was a Red Indian myself really. Ha ha. I was in a way. A loser. Somebody out of step, different.

The others were glad to be cowboys, but I tried to be and couldn't. It wasn't possible. I got a book from the library about the Native American tribes. It broke my heart when I learnt how they had been duped and treated and I cried when I saw the photo of thousands and thousands of buffalo skeletons strewn across the prairie. The white man did that to cut off the sources of food and shelter and clothing that Indians had lived on for generations. All them animals shot for spite. Oh, I did cry.

When did I give up trying? Trying to be like the others. That's a good question. I tried to fit in more when I realised how bad it was, getting knocked about all the time. At home, in school, everywhere. The hiding away didn't stop me getting hammered. Yes, while I was hiding I was all right, but sooner or later, I had to come out and I was back in trouble again. Thinking back, the only time I really enjoyed anything in my youth was when I was with that woman in the hut and with Miss Barton. My God, I enjoyed that, but in neither instance could it have lasted. I was bloody lucky to have what I did have at that age. And get away with it.

And what I did learn when I was growing up was to hide what I was thinking, what I was feeling inside. I needed to do that because of all the slaum I got from the family and Peg. After a short time being married to her I said very little, and never about my dreams of a better life.

'Don't be bloody daft, you're not right in the head. Do you know that?' she would keep saying.

Oh, and of course there was Jane. Loving her was a hopeless, hurting thing though. The possibility of something as beautiful and rare as that coming to fruition was a dream. Tommy Goodwin was never really going to be that lucky.

Jane was the only one who fully understood me, but I'm not certain how she would react to this plan. In this, what I'm going to do today, I am truly on my own. But then, apart from the little time spent with Jane, I always was.

I have done everything I can to make sure they can't blame any of this on the accident. All that did was to confirm things I already knew. That I was different from others and also that justice was a very selective process.

If I could have stayed with the pigs, the Landrace, I'm sure things would have been different. I loved them animals. People have no idea, none whatsoever about pigs. They are the most intelligent of creatures and not like what most people think. Give them room and care and they are as clean as human beings. What am I thinking? They are cleaner than some folk I know.

There was no justice there, at the Royal Show, when we only took that silver. If the gaffer had stuck to it for just a bit longer we would have been all right. Yes, he was losing money and he had depended on getting the gold that year, but I'm sure we would have done it the year after. They couldn't have cheated twice. Not two years running.

And I wouldn't have gone down the pit and I wouldn't have been in this bloody wheelchair but—— Oh, what's the use? Nobody can put the clock back, can they?

Yet I still can't think of myself as a failure, not as a complete loser. Perhaps if I could, then I would settle for how I am. For what I am.

Nothing but a bloody cripple. Ha, they don't say that now, do they? They say 'disabled'. Well when was I ever abled, eh? When were people like me abled?

I've listened to old men talking in Cowswell. When the pits were nationalised a lot of folk thought things would change in a big way, but they were wrong. The same schools were still there with the same teachers. The new politics didn't reach where we lived to give any of us an equal chance in life. The same pits were there with the same gaffers and the men were just as wary of stepping out of line as they had been under the old regime. The poor sods who lived in a pit house were the worst off. They couldn't open their mouths about anything. They were always frightened they would get thrown out of their homes. We were treated like dogs in our area, worse than some dogs. That's why it was easy to start the new breakaway union here in North Nottingham to break the strike. They knew what they were doing, Maggie Thatcher's bloody lot. And now, today, I know what I'm doing as well.

I'll get the flask out. This is one of the props I'm using to make me being here more natural. Some think I'm waiting for somebody. Well, ha ha, I am in a way. Fate, I think you could call it. That's what I'm waiting for and I have to get the timing right so it'll make the headlines in tomorrow's papers. The bit that fate decides is who else will be in the news. Lots of them will be involved, but the media will select the few who have a special appeal, kids and lovers, and families, and old people. I'm happy to leave that to somebody else. When the time comes I'll just make it happen and that's it.

'Oh, thank you, you're very kind. No, ha ha, I don't have sugar to put in; it's not good for your health. Ha ha. Thank you. Thank you, that's lovely. Bye.'

A man saw me struggling to get the top off the flask and poured the coffee for me. He'll have a tale to tell before the day's out. My God, he will.

I do think learning about the Red Indians, or Native Americans as they are called now, started off the way I feel about injustice. It is definitely not about anything that's happened to me personally because in some ways I've been quite fortunate. Even the accident provided me with a way to achieve something. It got me out of the bloody pit and I hated that almost as much as I hate being crippled now.

The voluntary sector, as they call it, has opened doors that I didn't know existed. I did a course on social history and that was a real eye opener. I had read some books before about how the system was rigged, but I had no bloody idea what we were up against. Being the only miner there, I did feel a bit isolated at first, but it's surprising how being paralysed evens things out with folk. There were all sorts of people there, on the different programmes. One thing I did learn was that people from different parts of society are all just as ignorant about certain things as I was. It's as if some of us live on different planets. When one chap in the re-hab place, who'd been damaged in a car crash, discovered I had got paralysed in a pit accident he started to talk to me. He was a somebody at the Coal Board and thought it would be good to meet a collier. He'd got no bloody idea. None. He thought we worked to the rules he had been taught about. He was divorced from reality. But how could he have known what our reality was. When I told him a few stories about how real life was for us, he was astonished and so I was careful to furnish him with the facts and stick to what exactly happened. He said he would have things investigated and I laughed. I told him that all the bad things had been well covered up and he'd need to buy a lot of ale to get the truth out of some of the people involved. The man said he would do that, but whether he did or not I don't know.

What I do know is no government did anything to change life for the people around me. Things went from bad to worse.

I did feel for the nurses and the social workers in that re-hab place. They do get some stick, the poor sods. What they did for me opened up a path to learn about things that I would never have learned in a normal life.

A normal life. I wonder what one of them is. Do all these people moving past me here live normal lives?

I've sat here lots of times, just sitting and watching. Some run to catch the train and some arrive early and sit with a sudoku or read the paper. I always want to approach them as they read the news and ask questions. What do you think about this, that, or the other? Would there be a massive difference between *Daily Star* readers and *Sun* readers and those who take *The Times*? I noticed that people read the *Mirror* and the *Independent* and the *Mail* but they take *The Times* and the *Telegraph*. I notice things like that I do.

I was a hider. Now I am a watcher. A watcher and a waiter. Soon I shall be a doer. A big doer.

If it was the plight of the Indians what started it, then by the time the Serbs sat shelling Sarajevo it was well cemented. My attitude, my philosophy, that's what I'm on about.

Who cared what was happening for . . . four years was it? Innocent people with little or no protection being killed for sport. That's what it was about, just for sport. Men would leave their jobs on a Friday to go up into the hills surrounding the city and become part-time soldiers. They'd sit and take pot shots at folk below, killing dozens and dozens, and as long as they didn't overdo it in one go, nobody cared. It was only when that shell landed in the market and killed a number all at once that the world started to object in a proper manner. I know somebody who wrote to his MP. It just happened to be Douglas bloody Hurd, the foreign secretary. I saw the reply justifying this country's lack of action. Mealy-mouth words that said bogger-all and didn't help a soul. I wrote to my Member of Parliament and got something the same. Maybe I should have done then what I'm going to do now. Maybe, I don't know. But I wouldn't have had the wheelchair and that is a big factor in the plan. That's what is going to make it work in a very spectacular way.

I have been meeting with a group of thinkers for the last ten years or so in the local institute and our branch of the U3A. One of the best things ever, the University of the Third Age, and I have enjoyed it, the discussions and putting the world to rights, and the interesting points that some of them put forward, points a bit academic that I wouldn't have taken into consideration. But during all that time, none of us did anything, well not really. You can't count going on demonstrations for different causes doing something when nothing comes of it. Not getting something done are you? That's part of the problem. The boggers let us have the freedom to protest and demonstrate as long as nothing is done to alter things. I think that is what they do to maintain the status quo, allow a certain level of dissent and that bolsters their contention that we all have the freedom to decide things. Well, they aren't fooling me any longer, and when I've done this event today, they will have their work cut out convincing folk that doing nothing is all right, because it isn't. Let the experts explain me away. I've never done anything to make a difference, a wasted life. Till now that is and now, at last, I'm going to be of use. A useful life. Ha ha.

That man's looking at me. I hope I haven't been thinking out loud. I don't want anybody to hear about this. They'll all know soon enough.

'Yes thank you, I'm okay. but thank you for asking. Yes, I dropped off for a bit, but I'm not here to catch a train, so it doesn't matter. I'm alright.'

There are kind people, see. He must have been watching me, but he'll not see anything I don't want him to see, I'm bloody sure of that.

The problem is nobody wants to actually do anything and so nothing gets done and nothing alters. That's why there is so much injustice in the world. No repercussions.

I have tried, over many years, to talk seriously to my two grandsons. They just don't want to know. 'It's your future I'm talking about,' I tell them, but they're not interested. They are both bright lads, but all they are interested in is these bloody fancy pocket telephones and com-bloody-puter games. Yes, they tell me they'll get into university, but what for? What to do? Play more computer games, I expect.

I think just a few people could make all the difference. If, that is, they did something. What I'm going to do will make a difference. If I didn't believe that with all my heart, I wouldn't be doing it. It's certainly not for any glory or personal benefit, is it? Indeed, there'll be those who put me down as a mad man. That's how the authorities will want to portray me, as a mad man with a grudge against society. Ha, I'm not bothered about any of that as long as there's some who stop to think. Ah, now that's the rub. How many who are led to think will do anything? That's the bloody question. We've all seen what thinking can do. Bogger all, that's what thinking does. You can sit and think all you like and it'll alter nothing. It's actions that count.

I don't want to move from here yet. I'm out of the draught and it's a good place to observe things. A few weeks ago one of the station staff brought me a mug of tea. I was touched when she said I shouldn't be here when it was so cold. She looked really concerned when I said it was better sitting here and getting cold watching the trains than being among a lot of miserable old pensioners. I was really pleased that I had been noticed, but I thought it was best to leave her thinking I was taking time out from an old people's home. I can't afford to be too sensitive at this stage, but I hope that woman isn't working here today. I was frightened to go and look. I didn't want to know. See, I'm as bad as others when it comes to facing up to some things. It's just that she was kind to me. But I mustn't do anything that might jeopardise my plan. Stay with it, Tommy, you stuck it out when you were trapped under all that rock-fall and you can do it now. This is the finest way you can make a difference. After a life that some would count as a failure you are now going to make your mark. You are not a failure until you stop trying and I've always tried. I never gave up altogether. Him, supposed to be my dad, said time and again, 'You'll never be any good while you've got an 'ole in your arse.' Well, I've still got one and we'll soon see what good I can do.

I do wonder what Miss Barton would think. She was one of my very special mentors when I was a kid. I try not to think about her and the other woman now. They wouldn't understand this sort of thing, the thing I'm intending. They thought life was for living and they nearly convinced me as well, but, oh well, that was a lifetime ago. All that was before I married Peggy and, as things turned out, it's a bloody good job I had some of the other while I was able to.

Its funny, this being paralysed, you still have feelings, but it's all in the brain. Like when some of them had lost an arm or a leg, they told me that you sometimes wanted to scratch an itch on the part that was missing.

After Jane came that once to see me when I got out of hospital I wrote a few words saying how I couldn't lumber her with damaged goods and she should make a life for herself. The lad said he'd make sure she'd get it without his mam knowing. They pretended that the bit of paper had fallen onto the mat and the lad said his mam picked it up and read it. I knew they were both lying. Jane sent me a card from Dover saying she had got a teaching job abroad and wished me well. Oh yes, Peg was delighted to show me that. She will be laughing on the other side of her face when the solicitor reads them my will.

I've made a lot of mistakes in my life, I know, but I am convinced this hank isn't one of them. Some will say it's a gesture, a futile one. But somewhere there will be somebody in a position to change things and they will say this is what that man Tommy gave his life for, so we'd better make what changes we can before this sort of gesture catches on.

One mistake I almost made was the tape. Ha ha, I spent bloody hours writing down what I wanted to say and then reading it onto an audio tape. It sounded like the ravings of a bloody madman. Then I pretended I wanted to make a video tape for my funeral and asked the grandsons if I could borrow their little recorder machine. That went bloody wrong. They insisted on operating the camera so I had to go through with it and made a tuppenny-ha'penny speech for them to save and play out on the day of my funeral. I looked terrible. I looked eighty, not fifty-five. A bloody wizened old man, whose teeth didn't fit proper, saying he hoped nobody would be too upset. You could hear them two boggers laughing in the background. Well, they won't laugh when they see the news on telly tonight and read the note.

Busiest time is around five, that's when it'll have the biggest impact, when the place is packed with folk coming and going. I'm well prepared. What did that nice couple teach us on that rehab course after the accident? 'Fail to prepare, prepare to fail.' That was it. Well, I'll not fail, that's a certainty. Better not move my legs too much though, I don't want things falling out for folk to see.

I sat here every day for a whole week once. I was holding a banner, trying to get attention to what was happening in the Middle East. I gave out a few of the leaflets I'd had printed, but nobody showed any interest in doing anything. It was an advantage though, being in the wheelchair, I knew that straight away.

I'm glad now I didn't accept the invite to visit that mosque. I thought about it and very nearly did, then I thought, if I do they can point the finger and say I was radicalised there. I didn't need a bloody mosque to radicalise me. My life did that without help from any organised religion. I would have liked to learn more about it though, the Moslem way. There's got to be something in a belief like that, a religion that makes people want to die for it. Can you see a Church of England worshipper wanting to die for a parish church? They used to say it was the Tory party at prayer, but what is it now?

I was taken on a trip to a Sikh Temple some months ago and that was a novel experience. You can see that their religion really does means something to them, but that's not to say it could ever mean anything to me. I expect that's a culture thing. They've got some and we haven't.

I want to be more like Thomas Paine, a citizen of the world, for all mankind. That's a big thing, isn't it? I think it is. He risked his life to bring a lot of justice to American and French people, but the boggers in Westminster made sure he didn't get to do much here, other than publish his pamphlets.

'What? Oh thank you, I didn't know I'd dropped it. I must have dropped off, had a snooze.' Bloody Norah, Somebody picked up my flask top. What time is it? Oh, I'm alright for a bit longer.

I've no regrets really. It would have been nice to have married Janey, but it wasn't to be and working this out at least I've found a purpose. Bit of a bogger though, getting the cancer in the part that's paralysed. It got a good start before anybody knew about it. Still, nobody lives forever, we all die of something. It's what you use your life for, that's what matters.

I thought about all that before this latest bother in the news. There's lots of new Red Indians struggling to exist. If you don't give them something to live for, they might well find something to die for. This is what's made up my mind really. The demonstrations against injustice around the world won't alter a thing, but a few like me might. What they call copycats. We'll see. Well, I won't see, will I? But somebody will. My grandsons will. See. See, if you can't make much of your life then it's what you use your death for that matters. Ah, I should have written that down.

Soon be time, five-ish.

He should be on the next train to come in. Just a minor official. They'll come past here, probably smiling, and that'll be it. Job done. Ah, he might walk over to shake hands. That'll be a laugh. I'd like that, to go out laughing, 'cause there's not been a lot to laugh at in my life.

Wonder what the lads will think of grandad. I've thought about that a lot because I'm doing this to make a better world for lads like them. The note in the post will be delivered tomorrow or the next day. Pushing that in the post box was when I made the final commitment. Mind you, it's to my address, so if it don't work there's a get out. Belt and braces man, that's me.

What's going on over there?

Sommat's up. Police. What do they want? Just sit tight Tommy and watch. It's nowt to do with me. They're moving folk away. Why are they doing that?

'Sorry, officer, what do you say? Clear the platform. What for? Who? Well he's nobody. He's with who? Well he is very important, I'd love to have a word with him. Can I not stay here, officer? It'll be photo opportunity for him. Please?'

Bogger. Bogger, bogger, bogger. I didn't think they would clear the station just because a petty bloody Yank was coming and they didn't let on a cabinet minister was bringing him either. Crafty bastards.

'Officer, why have we all got to move? Security? Can I not sit here out of the way?' Oh, all right, all right.'

Bogger. 'No, I don't need any help, thank you. I can manage to get myself home; I only live round the next street. Are you sure I can't stay? I just come here to sit and watch the trains. The staff here know that, just ask them.'

'Don't push so fast. I can leave under my own steam.'

It's hard to imagine now that this street would have been bloody thronged with police and press and telly people if it had worked out. I started taking more notice of the neighbours when I made the plan; if they were at home they'd have heard the explosion. I'm beginning to wonder now. Is this lot really worth dying for?

Ha. Here's the grandsons waiting for me outside the house.

'Have you come to see your daft grandad, lads? It's time you idle boggers got a job. You'll be out of uni. with a daft degree and unemployable before you know what bloody day it is. When I was your age, I'd been at work five years.

'Whoa! Steady with the chair lads, you'll tip me out. Stop larking about. No, don't pull that. No. No! No——'